STORM RUNNERS

ERUPTION

ROLAND SMITH

SCHOLASTIC PRESS
NEW YORK

Library of Congress Cataloging-in-Publication Data Available

ISBN 978-0-545-08174-0

10 9 8 7 6 5 4 3 2 1   12 13 14 15 16

Printed in the U.S.A.   23

First edition, March 2012

Book design by Phil Falco

DISCARD

FOR JOAN ARTH AND
NAOMI WILLIAMSON.
LOOK FOR THE TWO Ds.

THE ONLY EASY DAY
WAS YESTERDAY...

Chase Masters sat on a hay bale next to his father, John. His broken front tooth hurt, his shoulder ached, and he was exhausted but oddly content.

Not many people survive a Category Five hurricane, a bus sinking, a lion attack, a leopard capture, a torrential flood . . . oh, and a thirteen-foot alligator. *He shook his head in wonder.* And now we're heading to Mexico?

His father was staring at the elephant and its calf as they paced around the ring. Rashawn was scooping grain out of a fifty-gallon barrel. The Rossis were examining Momma Rossi's injured monkey, Poco. Cindy and Mark were reviewing the video footage Mark had just taken.

His father stood up and stretched. "I guess we'd better get moving. We have a lot of work to do before we head to the air-port." *He looked at Chase.* "Nine thirty?"

Chase looked at his watch.

"Exactly," *Chase said.*

Nicole, Marco, and Momma Rossi started arguing.

"Let's give them some privacy, Chase," John Masters said quietly. "Cindy, Mark — you too."

"We'll go out back and shoot some B-roll of the damage," Cindy Stewart said.

"Always thinking of your next story!" Cindy's cameraman, Mark, rolled his eyes. "That's why you're in front of the camera, and I'm behind it. Where did Richard go? Doesn't the Number One News Anchor in Saint Petersburg, Florida, want to take over this story too? I can see it now: 'Hurricane Emily: A Journey through the Aftermath with Richard Krupp.'"

"He headed home to see if his family is okay," John said. "That's why he came with us to Palm Breeze."

"Yeah, yeah, and to steal our hurricane footage," Mark said as he followed Cindy out the door.

"I guess I'll go to the bunkhouse to rustle up some food," Rashawn Stone said. "I worked up an appetite dodging that leopard. Can I borrow your satellite phone, Mr. Masters? I'd like to see if I can get ahold of my daddy."

John handed her his phone.

"We'll meet you at the truck," Chase told Nicole as he and his father headed to the far door.

Nicole stopped arguing with her father and grandmother just long enough to holler, "Remember Simba's locked in there!"

"Funny girl," Chase's father said. "I have no intention of getting the generators out of my truck until that lion is out of my rig. How big is he?"

"Big enough," Chase said, shuddering at the thought of seeing Simba again. He looked back at Nicole. The Rossis presented a strange sight. They stood at the edge of a dimly lit circus ring, an elephant with a newborn calf rattling her chains behind them. Nicole wasn't that tall, but she stood at least two feet taller than her father and grandmother. Marco and Momma Rossi were little people.

Outside the circus barn, it looked as if the world had been tipped upside down and shaken out onto the ground. Tomás was walking around the paddocks, talking on his satellite phone while he picked through the storm debris.

It was a beautiful Florida morning — warm, a slight breeze, not a cloud in the sky. If it weren't for the debris scattered everywhere, it would be hard to believe that Hurricane Emily had swept through a few hours earlier, grinding the community of Palm Breeze into splinters.

"Looks like you picked the best building to take shelter in," Chase's father said.

The circus barn was the only building on the property with minimal damage.

"It was luck," Chase said.

"Fate," his father said.

"What's the difference?"

His father shrugged.

"What now?" Chase asked.

"Tomás is talking to Arturo in Mexico City. We'll meet him there tomorrow and head south."

"What about Nicole?"

"She's welcome to come if she can talk her dad into it, but I wouldn't hold my breath. We're not going down there on vacation. I can't guarantee her safety, and neither can you."

"Nicole can take care of herself. I wouldn't count her out. She's tough."

"After what you, Nicole, and Rashawn lived through last night, I have no doubt about that." His father continued, "You don't have to come with us. I'm sure Mr. Rossi would be happy to put you up. There's plenty to do here, and he could use your help."

"You want me to stay?"

"No, but you've been through a lot over the past twenty-four hours."

"So have you."

The all-night trip to reach the Rossis' farm had cost John Masters two trucks and nearly his life. On the way, his partner, Tomás, had gotten a call from his brother, Arturo, in Mexico City. Arturo had driven a load of animals south of the border for the Rossi Brothers' Circus, but the circus hadn't been there to meet him and he'd been unable to reach them by phone. Arturo thought the show was stranded in the mountains outside of Puebla, close to the village where Tomás's wife and children lived. While Emily had been smashing Palm Breeze, a 7.5 magnitude earthquake had been crushing Puebla.

"It's your call," Chase's father said.

Chase wanted to say that he'd go if Nicole went, but whether she went or not was out of his control and, he had to admit, out of the question. He was going to Mexico.

"I'm in."

His father nodded.

"What about the reporters?"

"They're going too."

"Why?"

His father avoided Chase's gaze and looked toward the debris-ridden path. "I'm not exactly sure," he finally said. "I guess we got close during the hurricane. Extreme danger does that to people."

Chase had seen how Cindy Stewart looked at his father, and how his father looked at Cindy. As far as he knew, his father hadn't been on a single date since Chase's mother and little sister had died two years earlier. Chase didn't object to his father's new relationship, if that's even what it was. *It just feels a little sudden*, he thought. Less than forty-eight hours ago, his father and Tomás had headed off to Saint Petersburg to look for work. A few hours later, he'd seen his father on television being interviewed by Cindy about disaster preparedness. Then she showed up with his father at the Rossis' farm. Now she and her cameraman were going to Mexico with them? Chase was having a hard time wrapping his mind around it.

"Cindy's making a documentary," his father said.

"About what?"

"Hurricane Emily, for one thing. The earthquake in Mexico. Natural disasters . . ." His father hesitated. "And me, I guess."

"You?"

His father knew a lot about natural disasters and was an interesting guy. *But a documentary about him?*

"She was curious about me getting struck by lightning," his father said.

Chase was surprised to hear that his father had told someone he'd just met about the lightning strike. As far as he knew, his father had never told anyone. It had happened a year ago, in the backyard of their home. Chase had seen a blinding flash, and the next thing he knew, someone was giving his father CPR. His father was in a coma for two days. When he woke up, he sold everything they owned, including their home. Then he bought a semitruck to carry building supplies, and a fifth-wheel to live in. He and Chase and Tomás hit the road, running after storms, charging desperate victims a fortune to repair the damage. Chase looked at the gold lightning bolt earring in his father's earlobe.

Did he also tell her the bolt was made from his wedding band?

"It might help us to have a news crew from the States," his father continued.

"How so?" Chase asked.

"For Mexico to get aid, they need to get the word out about the earthquake. The news here is going to be about Hurricane Emily twenty-four-seven. Natural disasters compete with each other for money and airwaves. I think the officials in Mexico might be more lenient about letting us into restricted areas with a reporter and a cameraman on board. They need to get the word out."

His father was probably right. Chase and his father didn't watch a lot of television, but when they did, it was always weather and disaster related. They were well versed in the tragedy and politics of natural disasters.

"Just the opposite of here," Chase said. "How did you get past the roadblocks?"

"Tomás found a way around them."

"He always does."

Tomás — short, strong, and quick — hurried across the paddocks toward them, stuffing his sat phone into his back pocket. He had been working at Chase's father's side for over twenty years, and during that time, neither had mastered the other's language. They spoke in what could only be called Spanglish. Tomás was talking nearly as quickly as he'd been walking, but Chase was able to pick out a few words: *quads, compound, lion, generator, steel, winch, elephant, welder, dentist . . .*

The word *dentist* did not usually give Chase a jolt of joy, but today was different. He had snapped off one of his front teeth when the school bus sank. The broken tooth was killing him. The only way he could stand the pain was by keeping his upper lip wrapped around the jagged edge.

When the conversation ended, Tomás nodded and trotted off.

"Wait!" Chase winced as air hit his tooth.

Tomás stopped and looked back.

"Does he understand there's a lion in the semi?"

His father laughed. "Yeah, he understands." He waved Tomás on his way. "He's going to build a bridge across that gap."

The night before, during the worst of the storm surge, a river of water had roared between two of the barns, scooping out a deep furrow. Chase and Nicole had managed to wade across the gap twice. They had trapped Simba in the semi-trailer on the other side of the gap. Most of Chase's father's tools were in the semi, including the three industrial generators they needed to power up the Rossis' farm.

Chase and his father walked over to the gap. It was littered with debris, most of which, the day before, had been the Rossis' farmhouse.

"Is that a dead giraffe?" his father asked in shock.

"Gertrude," Chase said.

"Horrible," his father said.

Chase had already seen the dead giraffe and had paid his last respects. What now interested him was the storage container sitting crossways between the two barns. He stepped over Gertrude's neck to get a closer look.

"What is it?" his father asked.

"Momma Rossi was convinced Hurricane Emily was going to hit the farm. She has . . ." Chase hesitated. He didn't want to tell his father that Nicole's grandmother was a psychic, but she had certainly been right about the hurricane. "She was right."

"Lucky guess," his father said.

It was more than luck, Chase thought. "I loaded that container with boxes of Rossi Brothers' Circus memorabilia and other valuables. I caulked it and bungeed a tarp around it. The tarp's gone, of course, but it looks like . . ."

His father examined the container's seams and its door. He climbed underneath and checked the undercarriage. "You did a heck of a job, Chase. It looks like it rolled down here. Where was it parked?"

"Behind their house. Well . . . where the house used to be."

"A house can be rebuilt," his father said. "But the stuff inside the container is irreplaceable. You saved the Rossis' past."

Chase flushed. Praise was something his father did not give out easily, or often.

"If we have time, we'll try to pull the container out of here with the tractor." His father looked at the barn to their right. "What's in this one?"

"More animals," Chase answered. "Ostriches, zebras, parrots, and a bear named Brutus."

"Let's go check it out. Might be room to park the container inside."

"That's probably not a good idea until they get Brutus back into his cage."

"The bear's loose in there?"

"The last time I looked, yeah. Along with the ostriches, except for the one Nicole had to shoot after it broke its legs running into a wall."

His father shook his head. "You had a much more interesting night than I thought."

More terrifying than interesting, Chase thought, but didn't say it. "Why's Tomás building a bridge?"

"I thought it might be easier to get the lion out of the semi by backing it right up to the cat cage in the circus barn. Once we have the cat out of the bag, I can hook up the three generators in tandem without moving them out of the truck. We'll have enough power to run anything we need, including the arc welders."

"Why do you need the welders?"

"Because Marco told me that he doesn't have an elephant-proof barn. We're going to make it elephant-proof before we go to Mexico."

"When does our flight leave?"

His father smiled. "What time is it?"

The Internal Clock Game. Chase's father did not wear a watch. Since the lightning strike, he hadn't needed one. He always knew exactly what time it was — to the minute.

Chase looked at his watch. "You tell me."

"Ten-oh-two."

"Exactly."

"That gives us ten hours before we have to leave for the airport to catch the red-eye to Mexico City."

11:46 AM

The Rossis came out of the barn, followed by Rashawn, just as Chase, John, and Tomás were pounding the final nails into their bridge. Nicole was smiling, which could mean only one thing. She was going to Mexico.

"Against my better judgment," Marco began. "And because I've been outvoted two to one." He glanced at Nicole and Momma Rossi. "Nicole can go to Mexico with you if you'll have her. I'm hoping you'll say no."

Chase's father stood up and slipped his hammer into his tool belt. "Sorry," he said. "But it's your call, not mine."

"I had a feeling you were going to say that." Marco looked at his daughter and his mother. "When you see my wife in Mexico, tell her the reason I sent Nicole down there is that my mother is absolutely convinced that Nicole has to go, or bad things will happen. As if an earthquake isn't bad enough."

Chase's father climbed out of the ditch and looked at Momma Rossi. "What kind of bad things?"

"We need to check on the animals," Momma Rossi said, and walked toward the second barn without answering him.

As they followed, Chase's father stopped him. "What was that all about?"

"Momma Rossi, well . . . I don't know how to say it exactly. She can see things."

"She's psychic?"

"You'll have to ask her."

Food and security were all it really took to get the animals back where they belonged . . . along with some repairs. Chase's father and Tomás fixed the bear cage while Marco kept Brutus away from them by pounding a metal garbage-can lid with a stick. Next they fixed the ostrich pen while Nicole, Rashawn, and Chase corralled the birds into a corner by spreading their arms so the birds wouldn't run around and smash into walls. When the ostrich pen was repaired, Marco dumped some chow into their troughs. The ostriches couldn't get inside the pen fast enough. Brutus proved to be more of a challenge. He wasn't hungry, having eaten a good portion of the ostrich Nicole had been forced to shoot the night before. Marco was about to use the tranquilizer gun on him, when Momma Rossi walked in to see how things were going.

"No need for that," she said. "Brutus, get in that cage right now!"

Brutus looked up at her, with black feathers dangling from his mouth, but he didn't leave the bird carcass.

"Fine," Momma Rossi said, and rushed him. It was hard to say who was more startled, Brutus or everyone in the barn watching. She slapped him on the rear end. He bellowed in protest and nearly knocked Marco down in his desperation to get into his cage.

"Now, why didn't I think of that?" Marco said, shaking his head in dismay. "I can just see the headline now. 'Old Woman Killed by Bear After Surviving the Storm of the Century.'"

"You didn't think of it because you didn't raise Brutus from a cub. I did. He and I have an understanding."

"You raised me from a cub too," Marco said. "But I'm liable to bite you if you ever try to swat *me* on the butt."

Momma Rossi raised her hand. "Let's give it a try and see what happens."

"I wouldn't if I were you, Dad," Nicole said.

"You're probably right."

01:15 PM

A truck bearing the logo of the Palm Breeze Wildlife Refuge pulled up as they were walking over to the third barn to check on the lions.

"Daddy!" Rashawn threw her arms around the man who had just stepped out of the cab. He returned the hug, then picked her up and swung her around in a circle. Mr. Stone was a giant and looked strong enough to swing Brutus around too.

He reached over to shake Chase's hand. "You must be Chase. Rashawn tells me that if it hadn't been for you, she wouldn't have survived the storm."

"We helped each other," Chase said. "If we hadn't, none of us would have made it through Emily."

"However it went down, I'm grateful," Mr. Stone said. He gave Rashawn another hug and looked at Marco. "The name's Roger Stone. I manage the refuge down the road. I'm here to help in any way I can."

"Marco Rossi." Marco shook the tall man's hand. "Right now we're getting the animals contained. Four lions to go . . . five if you count Simba, but he's already kind of contained." Marco nodded at the semi.

"Rashawn told me about that on the phone," Roger said. "I don't know much about lions, but I've handled a lot of bobcats and pumas over the years."

They walked to the third barn, which had partially collapsed. The young lion and three lionesses were in the outside pen, which was in pretty good shape. The men made a few quick repairs to the chain-link fence and pulled the debris off the wire before going inside. The holding areas were completely destroyed, except Simba's cage.

"If the lions had been inside, they would have been crushed," Marco said.

"Or they would have escaped," Nicole added.

"Lucky," Marco said.

"Fate?" Chase asked his father.

"You'll have to ask Momma Rossi."

02:20 PM

Tomás jumped into the semi, pulled it across the new bridge, then backed it into the first barn. Pet trumpeted. Her calf took shelter between her legs. Hector the leopard growled and hit the bars of his holding cage. Even Poco, the injured squirrel monkey, weakly protested as the rig backed up toward the cat cage. Momma Rossi cradled Poco in her arm, trying to comfort him. Inside the trailer, Simba was silent. No roaring. No slamming into the walls as he had done the night before.

"You sure he's in there?" Marco asked.

"He's in there," Nicole said.

Chase wasn't as certain. Simba was being awfully quiet.

Tomás aligned the trailer perfectly with the section of cage they had removed. Marco had rigged a rope to the truck's door latch so it could be pulled from outside the cage, from the top of the trailer.

"Who wants to do the honors?" he asked, holding the end of the rope and a long pole.

"I'll do it," Roger said. "But you'll need to tell me what I have to do."

"Pretty simple. Get on top of the trailer, pull the rope to release the latch, use the pole to swing the doors open, and try not to fall inside the cage with Simba."

"I'll pay particular attention to that last part," Roger said.

"I'll work the holding-area door," Marco said. "Hopefully, Simba's hungry and will dash inside to get the meat."

Simba was out of the truck and into the cage before Roger was able to push the truck door all the way open. The cat roared, and rushed the bars of the circular cage, shaking the entire structure.

"He jumped over your heads last night?" Chase's father asked.

"Yeah."

"I would have had a heart attack."

"I think I did," Chase said, feeling his legs go weak at the memory.

Simba strutted to the center of the ring and let loose one final roar that echoed through the barn long after it had ended. He shook his black mane as if he was shaking off his rage, then caught the scent of the meat.

"That's it, old man," Marco said. "Dinnertime."

Simba growled, then sprinted into the holding area. Marco closed the guillotine door behind him.

"The animals are contained," Marco said with a sigh of relief.

It took them the rest of the day to elephant-proof the barn.

07:45 PM

Roger Stone had offered to drive them to the airport in the refuge's touring van. When he returned with the van, he had a couple of extra passengers: Rashawn's mom and two-year-old brother, Randall, who was a miniature version of Rashawn.

"Where's elephant?" he asked. "Show me elephant."

"I guess I'd better stick here with Randall," Rashawn said, laughing. "He'll throw a fit if we try to get him back in that van."

"There isn't enough room in the van for all of us anyway," Mrs. Stone said. "I'll stay here too. It takes two people to take care of Randall."

Chase and Nicole gave Rashawn hugs good-bye, promising to stay safe.

Chase and his father were the last ones to get into the van. Momma Rossi took John's hand and fixed her dark eyes on him.

"What?" John asked.

"That lightning is still looking for you," Momma Rossi said.

He gave her an uncomfortable smile. "It already found me."

She returned his smile. "It's going to find you again, Lightning John."

Before he could ask her what she meant, she hurried after Rashawn and Randall into the elephant barn.

John looked at Chase. "Did you tell her about the lightning strike?"

Chase shook his head. "No, nothing. But I like the name."

"I'm serious."

"I didn't tell her," Chase said. "Momma Rossi just knows things."

WEDNESDAY
10:00 AM

The high-pitched whine of the dentist's drill sent shivers down Chase's spine. He had slept soundly on the flight to Mexico, but he was awake now.

Wide awake, Chase thought.

The dentist asked him something in Spanish, which he didn't understand — not that he would have been able to answer anyway. His mouth was stuffed with clamps, spreaders, gauze, surgical-gloved fingers, and a nasty-sounding suction hose. He nodded, hoping the dentist hadn't just asked him if he wanted a gold tooth. The next sensation was almost as bad as the drill. It felt as if the dentist were pounding the cap on with a ball-peen hammer. The man finally finished, smiled, said something else Chase didn't understand, and started extracting the hardware from Chase's mouth. When he was done, he smiled again and handed Chase a mirror. To Chase's relief, his new front tooth was porcelain and a pretty good match to his other front tooth.

Nicole was waiting for him in the reception area.

"Let's see."

Chase smiled to show her, but he really wasn't sure if she could see the new tooth. He really wasn't sure if he'd even moved his mouth — his face was numb from his upper lip to the top of his forehead.

"Looks good," Nicole said.

Chase paid the dentist in cash. Before they'd left the Rossis' farm, his father had given him a pile of money. Chase had always wondered what his father did with the money he made repairing storm damage. Apparently, he kept it in cash — in large-denomination bills — inside his go bag along with the emergency supplies. They all carried go bags now, including Cindy and Mark, as well as new satellite phones so they could stay in touch without relying on cell towers.

"What did you learn?" Chase asked. He had given Nicole his laptop to keep while he was in the dentist's chair.

"A lot," Nicole said. "And none of it's good. Half of Puebla has been turned to rubble. Thousands of people are dead or missing. All the roads are impassable. They're using helicopters to get rescue workers in and the injured out, but it's very slow going. And to top it off, Mount Popocatepetl is smoking."

"Mount what?"

"Po-po-cat-uh-petal." Nicole pronounced it slowly. "It means 'smoking mountain.'"

"It's erupting?"

"Steam and ash, but nothing serious yet."

"This just gets better and better," Chase said. "What about your mom?"

Nicole shook her head. "No word. Their last performance was in Puebla, Monday night. Normally, they would have struck the show right after the final act and hit the road when the traffic was light. They were supposed to meet Arturo here in Mexico City yesterday to pick up the animals he was hauling down. The show is supposed to start tonight, and they aren't here. This is the first time in a hundred years that the Rossi Brothers' Circus has missed a performance."

"So they're stuck in Puebla, or just outside it."

Nicole gave him a worried nod.

"Don't worry," Chase said. "We'll find them. Where are my dad and Tomás?"

"Out getting supplies. Arturo's at the fairgrounds just down the street. We're supposed to meet everyone there."

10:35 AM

Arturo was an exact copy of Tomás, only younger and with a small chimpanzee on his lap. Nicole picked the chimpanzee up and gave it a hug. It seemed happy to see her.

"How was dentist?" Arturo asked.

Chase smiled and showed his new tooth.

"*Bueno.*"

Chase pointed at the chimpanzee. "What's his name?"

"It's a she, and her name is Chiquita."

Chiquita wasn't alone. There were two camels, a black bear, a tiger, and a good-size crowd of people gawking at the animals. Arturo had roped off the area to keep the spectators at a distance.

"You should charge an entrance fee," Nicole said.

"I'm thinking about it. They are here from morning until darkness. I have to pay children to bring me food."

Chase looked at Arturo's old sleeping bag and rumpled clothes in the back of the truck. Since meeting Nicole, he had thought more than once about becoming a circus roustabout when he got older. This sight took some of the romance out of the idea. Sleeping in the back of a truck without being able to leave to get food did not sound like much fun.

"I take it you're not coming with us," Nicole said.

"The only way I could go would be to take the animals with me. But of course that won't work. I'll wait here in case your mother shows up while you're out looking for her."

"The clowns will be happy to see Chiquita," Nicole explained to Chase. "Chiquita and her twin brother, Chico, are part of their act. Chiquita was under the weather when the show headed south, so we held her back. But you're all better now, aren't you, Chiquita?"

Chiquita gave her a hoot and a high five.

Two brand-new, white 4x4 trucks pulled up, equipped with crew cabs, roll bars, auxiliary lights, and power winches. Strapped down in the bed of each truck was a quad. The sides of both trucks were stenciled in red:

M.D. Emergency Services

The *M.D.* didn't stand for *Medical Doctor*, but sometimes the authorities thought it did and Chase's father didn't correct them. It helped get them into restricted areas. *M.D.* stood for *Masters of Disaster*. His father's little joke. But his father wasn't joking now. He climbed out of the truck all business. He didn't even ask about Chase's tooth.

"The new sat phones have GPS. Keep the phone with you at all times. I also got these." He handed Bluetooth earpieces to Chase and Nicole. Cindy, Mark, and Tomás already had theirs in. His father's Bluetooth flashed just above his lightning bolt earring.

That lightning is still looking for you, Momma Rossi had said. Chase wondered if the bolt had found his father while he'd been at the dentist's. John Masters looked completely charged — and clearly *in charge*. Chase smiled. *Lightning John is a perfect name for him.*

"The phones are synced to each other and will act like walkie-talkies," his father continued. "If you answer, you'll be able to hear everyone, and everyone will be able to hear you. Just tap the Bluetooth if you want to listen in. Mark and Cindy will ride with me. Chase and Nicole will ride with Tomás. When we get closer to Puebla, we'll decide our next step. And one more thing." He gave each of them a small zippered case. "Respirators in case we run into ash up on the mountain. Put them in your go bags. Any questions?"

No one had any questions. Or if they did, they didn't ask out loud. Mark was filming the whole thing. *That's a question killer*, Chase thought. *Who wants to ask a dumb question with the camera rolling?*

Tomás gave Arturo a hug and got into his truck. Chase and Nicole climbed in after him. Chase looked back as they drove away. His father was already getting into his truck behind them. Arturo was waving. Chiquita had her hand up too.

"Was your dad in the military?" Nicole asked as they pulled onto the highway.

"Navy," Chase answered. "But it was before he married my mom."

"What did he do in the Navy?"

"I never asked him, and he never talks about it. Why?"

"He seems . . . I don't know. Organized, I guess."

"He's certainly organized. Most contractors are."

"Circus people are organized too," Nicole said. "But your dad's *extra*-organized. We've been here less than five hours and he's mounted a full-scale expedition inside a foreign country."

"Mexico is hardly a foreign country."

"Look at this truck and all this special gear. He had to get a car dealer out of bed at the crack of dawn to get these trucks."

Chase looked around the cab. It smelled new. The only things that weren't new were the laminated photos of Tomás's eight children and his wife, Guadalupe, duct-taped to the dash. Above them was Tomás's plastic statue of Saint Christopher, patron saint of travelers.

He's also invoked against lightning, Chase thought. *Not a problem today. There isn't a cloud in the sky. People are driving, shopping, going about their day as if —*

"Popocatepetl," Tomás said.

The "smoking mountain" was smoking. A plume of white steam rose ten thousand feet above the nearly eighteen-thousand-foot peak.

"I didn't realize it was so close to Mexico City," Chase said.

Nicole turned and said something to Tomás in what sounded to Chase like pretty good Spanish. Tomás responded, and they continued speaking rapidly as the volcano loomed larger in the distance.

When they stopped talking, Chase asked Nicole about her Spanish.

"Circuses are international," Nicole said. "The acts are from all over the world, but most of our roustabouts are Hispanic. I was asking Tomás about his family. They live in a village called Lago de la Montaña, or Lake of the Mountain. I guess people call it Lago for short. It's on the east side of the mountain just below the rim."

"So, not a good place to be right now," Chase said.

"No," Tomás said.

They drove on in silence.

12:00 PM

"Noon," his father said over the Bluetooth.

Chase looked at his watch. "Exactly."

"Pull over where the road splits."

Tomás pulled the 4x4 onto the shoulder. Everyone got out.

"We haven't seen another car in half an hour," Chase's father said. "My guess is nobody's getting in or out of Puebla, at least not on this road. And I don't like the look of that plume. We need to split up so we can cover more ground. I'll continue toward Puebla and see what we're up against. Tomás will head up to Lago and make sure his family's okay."

"Then I want to ride with you, to Puebla," Nicole said to John.

"I figured that." He looked at Cindy and Mark. "One of you needs to go with Tomás and Chase."

"I'll do it," Cindy said. "Mark needs to shoot video. I'm extra baggage."

Except for Tomás and Lightning John, we're all extra baggage, Chase thought. He would have preferred to travel with Nicole, but he understood her wanting to go to Puebla, where her mother and sister might be. And he understood his father's reason for going to Puebla right away. The plume — what they could see of it now so close to the mountain — had turned from white to gray in the last half hour. Tomás had told them that didn't necessarily mean the volcano was going to be a problem. The steam and ash were common. But Chase could tell he was worried about it.

Nicole and Cindy went to pick up their go bags.

John waved Chase over to the guardrail to talk to him alone.

"You okay with Nicole going with me?"

"You okay with Cindy going with me?" Chase asked.

His father grinned. "Actually, I am. Take care of her, and take care of yourself."

"What do you want us to do when we find Tomás's family?"

He looked up the mountainside. "It's up to Tomás, but I'd get them out of here. I just really don't like the look of that plume."

"Do you know anything about volcanic eruptions?"

"A little. I was in a bad eruption in Indonesia before you were born."

"When you were in the Navy?"

His father nodded.

"Why were you in Indonesia?" This trip down to Mexico was Chase's first time out of the country, but apparently it was not his father's.

"I was sent there to help rescue some people."

"From an eruption?"

"Not exactly. Look — let's talk about this another time. We need to get moving."

"Sure," Chase said. *Just another thing he doesn't want to talk about.*

He walked over to Nicole. "Don't do anything I wouldn't do."

She burst out laughing. "It can't be worse than the hurricane," she said.

Chase looked up at the gray plume. He wasn't so sure.

12:22 PM

"The bridge is out," John said.

There were three army trucks parked on their side of the bridge and no vehicles on the Puebla side. He slowed to a stop, then consulted his GPS.

"I'll go talk to them," Nicole said.

"I'll go with you," Mark said.

"Ask them when the bridge went out," John said, pulling a topographical map from the glove box to compare to the map on his phone.

The bridge had spanned a deep gully three hundred feet across. A third of the bridge was now gone. Nicole asked the soldiers when it had collapsed, but they didn't know exactly. They'd been sent from Mexico City right after the earthquake hit. When they called in and reported that the bridge was out, their commander told them to stay put until they were relieved. The sergeant asked if Nicole had any spare food or water. She sent Mark to see what Mr. Masters could spare.

"Did you see any circus trucks drive up to the other side? Or did you pass any circus trucks on your way up here?" Nicole asked in Spanish.

The sergeant shook his head. But he had heard about the circus. His cousin had gone to see it in Puebla. He'd been planning to take his family when the circus performed in Mexico City.

"That may not happen," Nicole told him. She went on to explain her connection to the circus and gathered as much information from the man as she could.

A few minutes later, Mark and John walked up with a box of food and water and handed it to the soldiers. Nicole filled them in. "The sergeant thinks my mother and sister and the rest of the circus probably started out of Puebla, found they couldn't get far on the ruined roads, and turned back. So maybe they're safe." *Or stranded somewhere on the road — or worse*, she thought. She continued aloud, "He says there are several roads and trails through the mountains, but they're only passable with four-wheel drive."

"I think I've found a way around the bridge," John said. "Ask him about the volcano."

"I already did," she told him. "He said the same thing as Tomás. He isn't worried about Popocatepetl either. He told me the mountain lets out steam all of the time, and it's nothing serious. He's guessing the earthquake opened a fissure in the crater, but it will close up in a couple of days. It always does, he said."

John gave the sergeant his phone number and asked him to call if he heard anything about the circus or warnings about the volcano. Back in the truck, he showed Nicole and Mark the map, moving his finger along the road he was planning to take.

"It looks more like a trail than a road," Mark said.

"It is a trail," John admitted. "It swings back around to the highway on the other side of the bridge. If it's wide enough and not too steep, we should be able to make it."

"If it's still there after the earthquake," Mark said.

John put the truck into four-wheel drive. "If the trail's not there, we'll make our own."

Mark rolled his eyes. "Here we go again."

"What are you talking about?" Nicole asked.

"When we ran out of roads during the hurricane, Lightning John here and his sidekick, Tomás, decided to redefine the meaning of *off-road vehicle*. At one point we were stuck on a train trestle. I can't tell you how much fun that was."

John smiled. "Lightning John, huh? I gather Chase told you? It's not the worst nickname I've had." He bumped the truck off the highway and headed into the trees.

12:33 PM

In some ways Popocatepetl reminded Chase of Mount Hood. The dense blanket of evergreen trees, the steep and winding logging roads, the small patches of snow surviving in the shade. Before the lightning strike — before everything changed — his family had owned a cabin on Mount Hood. They had spent almost as much time at the cabin as they did in their regular home. His father had even been a volunteer in the Mount Hood Ski Patrol. Chase's best memories were from their time on the mountain. His worst memory was too.

"So tell me something about Chase Masters," Cindy said. She was sitting between him and Tomás.

"There's not much to tell," Chase said.

Cindy laughed. "You sound like your dad."

"You sound like a reporter."

"Guilty as charged. It's in my blood. My parents are both journalists."

"Where do they live?" Chase asked.

"Southern California. In the same house I grew up in."

"So you know about earthquakes."

"I've been in my share of quakes, and of course I've covered them for television."

"How about volcanoes?"

"The only volcano I've covered is Mount Saint Helens in Washington. I did a story about it the last time it acted up. It blew some steam and ash for a few days, then went back to sleep. I hope Popocatepetl does the same."

Chase hoped so too, but his TGB was telling him otherwise. How often had his father said, "The gut barometer is never wrong, so always listen to your TGB." His father believed that everyone had a TGB. It worked like a real barometer, but instead of hanging on a wall, it was in your solar plexus. "When you feel the bottom drop out of your gut, you'd better go on full alert," his father always said. Right now Chase's gut was somewhere between his knees and his ankles. He hoped the feeling of hollow dread was an aftereffect of the novocaine. *Or maybe I'm just hungry.* He hadn't eaten anything since the airplane. He pulled an energy bar out of his go bag and offered half to Cindy.

"No, thanks. Let's get back to Chase Masters."

"Like I said, there not much to tell. I was born and raised in Oregon. Two years ago, my mother and sister were killed in an auto accident. One year ago my father was struck by lightning in our backyard. When he came out of the coma, he sold my uncle his share in their construction company, and we hit the road. I go to school while my father and Tomás charge people a lot of money to put their property back together."

"I was sorry to hear about your mom and sister," Cindy said. "I can't imagine how difficult that's been."

"Thanks."

"As far as your father charging people a lot of money to fix things, I suspect he's spent most, if not all, of his profit on this little excursion. If he didn't have the cash, we'd be back in Florida, worrying about Tomás's and Nicole's families instead of down here trying to find them."

Chase shrugged. She had a point, but his father was not a psychic like Momma Rossi. He hadn't been charging people because he knew that one day he would have to save Tomás's and Nicole's families.

"I can see you're not convinced," Cindy said. "It's hard for men like your father to give up their training."

"What training?"

"His SEAL training."

"As in sea, air, and land? The Navy SEALs?"

"That's right."

"My father was not a Navy SEAL."

"Chief Petty Officer John Sebastian Masters."

"Sebastian?"

"Don't tell me you didn't know your father's middle name."

"I knew the initial," Chase said, which sounded weak even to him. "Did he tell you he was a Navy SEAL?"

"No."

"Then how —"

"You don't really think that I would pick your dad as a documentary subject without doing some research first?"

"I guess not," Chase said. *How could I not have known something so important?*

"My little brother — well, not so little anymore — is a Navy SEAL. We lived close to Coronado, California, where SEAL Team One is based. I can't remember a time when my brother didn't want to become a SEAL. His bedroom was plastered with SEAL paraphernalia and Navy recruiting posters. Your father was younger in the photo, of course, but I recognized him from one of those posters. I called my brother to verify it. He said John Sebastian Masters is the real deal. Your dad's exploits in Asia are the things of SEAL Team One legend."

Chase's father's voice echoed in his head. *I was in a bad eruption in Indonesia before you were born. . . . I was sent there to help rescue some people. . . .* Chase still couldn't believe he hadn't heard any of this before now. His mother had to have known his father had been a SEAL.

"What kind of operations?" Chase asked.

"My brother wouldn't tell me, the little creep. He said they were classified."

Chase looked over at Tomás. He had both hands on the steering wheel and was looking straight ahead as if he wasn't paying the slightest attention to their conversation. Did he know about his partner's past?

"What did my dad say when you asked him about being a SEAL?"

"I didn't ask him."

"Why not?" If they weren't driving up the side of an active volcano, he'd be on the sat phone with his father right now demanding an answer.

"Good question," Cindy said. "I guess I was waiting for him to say something about it, but the fact that he didn't tells me even more about him than if he had."

"How so?"

"I know a lot of ex-SEALs. They're a proud bunch and delighted to talk about their accomplishments. Then along comes someone like your dad, who doesn't even tell *you* about it. I assumed that you knew. I probably shouldn't have said anything."

"I'm glad you did," Chase said. "And don't worry. When I ask him about it, I'll figure out a way to do it without pointing at you."

"I'd appreciate that." Cindy looked out the windshield at the darkening sky. "The only easy day was yesterday," she said.

"What do you mean?"

"That's the SEAL motto."

Chase hoped it wasn't true.

12:52 PM

"Stop the truck!" Nicole shouted.

"Why?" John asked.

"Because I need to puke," Mark said.

"I'm serious," Nicole insisted. "I saw something!"

John put the brakes on, and Nicole was out of the cab before the truck came to a complete stop.

"I'm serious about puking," Mark said.

"Take care of it *outside* the cab while I find out what Nicole is up to."

The trail they had been following was slippery and narrow. They had already gotten stuck twice, but both times John had managed to get the truck loose without using the winch. He caught up to Nicole fifty yards into the woods, on the downhill side of the trail.

"What did you see?"

"I'm not sure." Nicole scanned the thick trees. "It was just a glimpse of something or someone."

"We're at least a mile above the highway and several miles from the nearest village. It's not likely that anyone would be wandering this far above the —"

The ground shook. John grabbed Nicole and pulled her down to the base of a tree, shielding her from the dead branches raining down. The tremor sounded like a freight train barreling right past them. John counted the seconds. When he reached nine the tremor stopped, followed by complete silence, as if the forest were holding its breath, waiting.

"You okay?" he asked.

"I think so." Nicole sat up and brushed the pine needles out of her black hair.

John looked up the hill and shouted, "Are you alive, Mark?"

"Barely!" Mark shouted back. "Oh, no . . ."

The ground had started shaking again.

The truck continued to shake *after* Tomás had stopped. Saint Christopher and two of Tomás's children fell off the dash. Four cracks appeared in front of the truck, as if a giant, invisible cat paw had scratched the road.

"Whoa," Chase said.

"I think that was the second tremor," Cindy said. "We couldn't feel the first one because the truck was moving."

Tomás put Saint Christopher back on the dash and replaced the photos of the two children. Everyone got out of the cab to take a closer look at the cracks.

"Not too bad," Tomás said. "We can get around them."

All at once, each of their satellite phones starting ringing. Chase was about to hit talk when he remembered the Bluetooth in his ear and tapped it instead.

"Are you guys okay?"

Chase jumped when he heard his father's voice directly in his ear.

"We're fine," Cindy said. Chase could hear her speaking out loud and in his ear at the same time. He walked a short distance away to avoid the echo. "There are some cracks in the road, but Tomás thinks we can get around them. Where are you?"

"About twelve miles from the bridge overland. An hour and a half by road. The bridge was out. We're trying to get around it and drop back down to the highway. It's tough going, but we're making progress."

"How's Nicole?" Chase asked.

"Shaken," Nicole answered in his earpiece.

Chase laughed. It was going to take him a while to get used to the fact that everyone was listening in.

"Nicole thought she saw something in the woods, so we stopped. Lucky we did. The truck slid about five feet during the last tremor. I'm going to have to winch it back up onto the trail."

"Don't worry about Mark," Mark chimed in. "He was crushed by the truck, but it means more food for all of you."

It was Cindy's turn to laugh. "Did you get video?"

"Of my death? Yeah."

"Good. Seriously, are you okay?"

"I'm fine. I was on the other side of the truck when it slid off the trail. And the camera *was* rolling. So were my bowels."

"Too much information, Mark."

"Don't worry. I didn't get any footage of that. You did hear that I said *trail* instead of *road*, right?"

"I heard."

"Lightning John is up to his old tricks, blazing trails like Meriwether Lewis. Why are we down here again?"

"We won't know until it's over," Cindy said.

"Perfect."

"We'd better get going," John interrupted. "We have to winch the truck back up, contact Mark's next of kin, then bury him."

"I think the mountain is going to take care of that for you," Mark said.

Lightning John laughed and ended the call.

01:06PM

"Landslide," Tomás said. When he spoke in English, it was usually in one-word sentences.

"A huge landslide," Chase said. A fifteen-foot pile of boulders and uprooted trees covered the road.

"How far is Lago?" Cindy asked.

"Nine or ten miles."

They got out of the truck. Chase started to climb the pile.

"What are you doing?" Cindy called after him.

"Checking to see how far it goes."

"Be careful."

"Yes, Mo — uh . . . ma'am. I'll be fine." *Did I almost say mom?* He scrambled up the loose scree as if he were trying to get away from the idea. *What's up with that?* He reached the top and looked at the debris pile. It was extensive. Fifty yards, maybe more. It would take a road crew a week to move it. A dangerous job. They'd have to start at the top of the slide and work their way down. *If the pile shifted, or if there was another earthquake . . .* Chase suddenly realized the precarious position he was in and quickly climbed back down.

"What's it look like?" Cindy asked.

"It's a mess. We're not getting past it, and no one from Lago is either. We were lucky we weren't driving by when this let go. I couldn't see very far beyond the slide, but there might be more slides up ahead. We're going to have to go around."

Chase looked at Tomás to see how much he had understood. Apparently, he'd understood enough, because he'd switched on his sat phone and was consulting the GPS. When he finished, he showed the screen to them and traced the alternate route he wanted to take. All of it was off-road.

"It might be best if we unload the quad," Chase said. Tomás nodded. "I can ride up ahead of you and make sure the path is clear."

"Crank the steering wheel to the left," John told Mark. "Keep your foot off the brake. When I tell you, give it a little gas. But don't let the wheels spin. If it starts to slide, we'll lose the truck. In fact, we should unload everything in case we do lose the truck. That way we'll still have the quad and our supplies."

"How many people can ride on the quad?" Mark asked.

"Two."

"But there are three of us."

"If we lose the truck, there won't be because you'll be inside the truck." John pointed down the steep hill. "Wherever it ends up."

"Maybe Nicole would like to do the truck thing."

"I'd be happy to," Nicole said.

"Except I told her dad that I'd try to keep her safe," John said.

Mark pulled his phone out of his pocket. "Wanna call my dad?"

John smiled. "Give me a hand unloading the quad."

"I'm going to look around," Nicole said. "I know I saw something."

"Don't wander too far," John said. "And take your go bag with you."

Nicole walked back to where she thought she had seen something. *Whatever it is*, she thought, uncertain why *it* was so important. *Mr. Masters probably thinks I'm insane.* She had seen *it* out of the corner of her eye past Mark's head on the passenger side. By the time she'd leaned forward, *it* had vanished into the trees. She scanned the forest for a familiar landmark. *There!* An old tree blown over by the wind or downed by lightning. She walked toward it. Halfway there, she saw a movement behind the splintered stump and stopped. She knew better than to walk up to a wild animal in the woods, if that's what it was. She waited and watched. In the distance she heard the truck start and John shouting instructions to Mark. *It* moved again. A humanlike face peered out from behind the stump. *It* was Chico, Chiquita's twin brother. He was baring his teeth in a fear grimace. She didn't blame him. Earthquakes were scary. So was being lost in the woods and separated from the show. She couldn't imagine what was going through the young chimp's mind, but she knew exactly what was going through her own.

Chico's bizarre appearance here meant that her mother and sister had to be nearby. It also meant that animals had escaped from the circus trucks, and the show was almost certainly in trouble. Nicole sat down on the ground and averted her gaze to make herself appear less threatening. If it had been Chiquita peeking out from behind the stump, Nicole would have walked up to her with open arms, calling her name, but she didn't know Chico that well. If she walked toward him, he was liable to run away. The only thing to do was wait for him to get over his fear and approach her.

If only I had some food, I could . . . She remembered the go bag. Very slowly she slipped the small backpack off her shoulders. Chico watched her suspiciously but didn't run. He showed a little more of his body as she unzipped a side pocket and pulled out an energy bar.

"Hungry?"

Chico stepped completely out from behind the stump.

"Me too." Nicole started to unwrap the bar. Chico took a tentative step forward. "You recognize my voice, don't you?"

Chico gave her a quiet woot.

"That's what I thought." Nicole took a bite out of the bar, then held the rest out to him. "You want some?"

"*Woot.*"

"You're going to have to come and get it, because I'm not bringing it to you. And you'd better make it quick. This train's about to leave the station."

Chico took a couple steps forward.

"I know you're scared. It's creepy when the ground shakes. Scared me too. But you're lucky you weren't at the farm during the hurricane. Now, *that* was terrifying."

Chico started knuckling his way toward Nicole, then froze, looking at something behind her.

"It's okay, Chico. Don't run off." Nicole turned her head. Mark was fifty feet away with his camera.

"Is that a chimpanzee?"

"No, Mark, it's a baby Sasquatch."

"Funny. Can I get a little closer?"

"No. You need to back off. Preferably all the way to the truck."

"I'm filming. You look just like Jane Goodall. This will be great for our —"

"Mark. You. Need. To. Get. Out. Of. Here. Now."

"I guess I'll get out of here," Mark said.

Nicole turned back around, half expecting Chico to be behind the stump again or, worse, completely gone. But he was still there, looking past her, watching Mark's retreat.

"Where were we?" she said. "Oh, yes . . . food." She pulled more of the wrapper away from the bar. Chico took another couple steps forward, reaching out for the treat. "No snatch-and-run for you. You're going to have to eat it here." She patted her lap.

"*Woot.*"

"That's right."

Reluctantly, Chico climbed into her lap. Nicole broke off a small chunk of energy bar and handed it to him.

"I wish you could talk and tell me what happened. Where are my mother and sister?"

"*Woot.*"

02:15 PM

Chase stopped the quad and waited for Tomás and Cindy to catch up. They had dropped below the slide and had managed to get past it without mishap.

Now the hard part.

He looked up the hill. It was a half-mile climb back up to the road, with no guarantee there wouldn't be more slides blocking their way to Lago. Chase's eyes stung and his mouth was dry from what he thought was dust. As the truck bounced toward him through the trackless forest, he saw that Tomás had his wipers on. The windshield was streaked with a gray slurry the color of cement.

Not dust. Ash.

Tomás and Cindy got out of the truck. Tomás opened the crew cab door and pulled out a roll of toilet paper.

"*Azufre,*" Tomás said.

Chase looked at Cindy. "Toilet paper?"

"I think *azufre* means 'brimstone,'" Cindy explained. "He's talking about volcanic ash. I have no idea why he has the toilet paper."

Tomás popped the hood, removed the air filter, and shook out a cloud of gray ash. He wrapped the filter in toilet paper, put it back in, then did the same to the air filter on the quad. He handed the toilet paper roll to Chase.

"Wrap every ten miles or the quad, it will stop."

"Sure." Chase put the roll in his go bag and pulled out his respirator.

"You need something for your eyes," Cindy told him.

Tomás ran to the back of the truck, rummaged through the toolbox, and came back with a pair of eye protectors and a roll of duct tape. He covered the perforated sides of the glasses with tape and handed them to Chase.

"Thanks."

"*De nada.*"

"I think you should stay down here with the truck while I go up and check the road to see if there are any more landslides." Chase took the sat phone out of his pocket. "I'll call you if it's clear."

Tomás nodded.

Cindy looked doubtful.

"There's no point in driving the truck up to the road if it isn't clear." Chase took his helmet off so he could put on the mask and the glasses. He had to leave the Bluetooth in his pocket because the helmet wouldn't fit over it.

"I just don't like the idea of us splitting up."

Chase put his helmet back on. "I've been driving a quad since I was five years old."

"But not during an eruption. I'm worried about this ash."

Chase was too. He looked up through the trees. It had gotten darker in the last hour, and the gray against the sky was not a thundercloud.

"It won't take me long." Chase swung onto the quad and started up the hill toward the road.

Nicole walked up to the truck with Chico in her arms. The young chimp was happily munching his third energy bar.

"I told you there was a chimp," Mark said.

"So you did," John said.

"Chico," Nicole said. "Chiquita's twin brother."

"Where does Chico ride when the circus is traveling?"

"In the clown truck."

"Semi?"

Nicole nodded. "Two drivers. They haul most of the wardrobe for the show, portable dressing rooms, props. The clowns follow the semi in campers and trailers."

"What are the chances of Chico's getting loose on his own?"

"Just about zero. When he's not performing, he's in a harness with a leash."

"No harness," Mark said.

"They take it off when they put him in his cage."

"Then we can assume the clown truck has had an accident," John said. "What other animals would the circus be transporting?"

"Lions, tigers, bears, camels, elephants, and dogs."

"Dogs?" Mark asked.

"Thirty-two of them. Mostly poodles. Teacup up to standard. It's the show's most popular act."

"How far can a chimp travel in a day?" John asked.

"I don't know. What worries me is, why did he travel anywhere?"

02:46 PM

Chase made it back up to the road, but it hadn't been easy. It was going to be even harder for the truck, but if anyone could get it up there, Tomás could. The road was covered with half an inch of fine gray ash. Sweat dripped down the back of Chase's neck from his helmet. He took it off, pulled down his respirator, took a long drink of water, then rinsed the ash off the safety glasses. The glasses had helped, but the stinging ash was still finding its way into his eyes. He put the Bluetooth back into his ear and hit redial on the sat phone. Cindy answered first.

"Are you on the road?"

"Yes. A lot of ash up here. I'm going to drive down a mile or so and make sure there aren't any more landslides. So stay put. I'll give you a call when I know."

"What landslides?" His father's voice was in his ear.

Chase had forgotten again that everyone could listen in. He told his father — and everyone else — about the landslide and their plan to get around it.

"How much ash is up there?" his father asked.

"Half an inch on the road. But it's not falling. It's kind of swirling around in the breeze."

"Same here," his father said. "There might have been an eruption *and* an earthquake. You need to get up to Lago. The sooner we get off this mountain, the better."

Chase could tell by the tone of his voice that his father's gut barometer was on high alert. Chase's TGB was too. The afternoon light filtering through the suspended ash was ghostlike. *I wonder if this is what it would look like after a nuclear explosion*, he thought.

"Are you wearing your respirator?" his father asked.

"Yeah. And some eye protection Tomás rigged up."

"Keep a lookout for circus animals," Nicole said.

"What?"

"I found Chico wandering around in the woods."

"The chimp?"

"Yes. He was scared to death. I don't know if any other animals escaped. Or if they did, whether they're anywhere near you. But it's possible. We looked at the map, and Chico was three miles from the highway."

"What other kinds of animals are you talking about?"

"Lions and tigers and bears, oh my," Mark said. "Along with some other less aggressive things."

Chase switched over to the phone's GPS screen. He was probably less than five miles from the highway as the crow flies. *Or as the tiger runs.*

"The only easy day was yesterday," he said.

"What did you say?" his father asked.

"I gotta go."

Chase ended the call, pulled the Bluetooth from his ear,

and put on his gear before getting back on the quad. He continued down the road, smiling. *Let* him *think about what* I *said for a change.* But the smile didn't last long. He rounded a corner and put on the brakes so hard, the quad nearly flipped. Sitting in the middle of the road was a gray poodle the size of a small domestic cat. At least, Chase thought it was a poodle, from the way its fur was cut.

And very few wild animals have blue bows tied to their ears.

The poodle was holding up its right front paw as if it were injured. If Chase hadn't slammed on the brakes, he would have run right over the tiny dog. He got off the quad, squatted down, and called the dog to him. The poodle didn't move.

"You probably think I'm an alien," Chase said. He took off his helmet, glasses, and respirator. "Is that better?" The poodle still didn't move. "Apparently, it isn't better. Look. We're on an active volcano. We need to get —"

The ground started shaking violently. Chase dropped to the ground and covered his head with his arms, wishing he'd kept his helmet on. The upheaval and deafening roar seemed to go on forever. When it finally stopped, Chase was still shaking even though the ground was still. As he struggled to catch his breath, he felt something rubbing against his thigh. He glanced down. The trembling poodle looked up at him. Chase picked up the dog and settled it in his lap. He started to pet it and discovered that the poodle was not gray. Its white fur was covered in ash.

03:04PM

John Masters felt the steering go and hit the brakes. The truck slid sideways for twenty feet before it slammed against a tree, crunching the passenger door. The ground continued to shake for a couple more seconds, then stopped.

Chico had his arms around Nicole's neck so tightly, he was nearly choking her. "That was a bad one," she said.

Mark rubbed the bump on his forehead. "I'm getting a little sick of these earthquakes!"

John was getting sick of them too, but this last one had felt a little different. "That might have been an eruption."

"Perfect," Mark said.

"Are you okay?" Nicole asked Mark.

"Just a small concussion. But thanks for asking."

"I'll check the truck." John put on his respirator.

"I'll go with you," Nicole said.

John shook his head. "You two stay here. No use in all of us going out into the ash."

With difficulty Nicole managed to peel Chico's arms from around her neck. They were less than half a mile from the highway. She hoped there was nothing wrong with the truck.

We're so close! she thought.

Her phone and Mark's rang simultaneously. Nicole put hers on speakerphone so she and Mark could listen together.

"Is everyone okay?" John asked.

"Tomás and I are fine," Cindy said. "We're waiting to hear from Chase."

"I'm fine," Chase said. "Tomás and Cindy, the road looks clear, so you can start making your way up here. Are you listening in, Nicole?"

"I'm here."

"Does the show have a dog act?"

"Yes. Why?"

"I think I have one of the performers in my lap. It's the size of a big squirrel."

"White?"

"It was, but now it's ash gray. It has blue bows in its ears."

"Pepe," Nicole said. "What's he doing all the way over there? Why is he loose? Why is he by himself?"

"I have no idea. I'm just glad it was Pepe in the middle of the road and not a lion, tiger, or bear."

"Oh, my," Mark said.

"Funny," Chase said. "I'm going to head up the road with Pepe and find out where he came from, or get to Lago, whichever comes first. Are you on the highway?"

"No," Nicole said. "We just hit a tree. I'm not sure if we're going anywhere."

"The truck's fine," John said. "Just a little dented. We'll be back down to the highway within half an hour unless we have another earthquake, or eruption. Everyone stay in touch." He ended the call.

Chase picked up Pepe and looked at the little poodle's paw. The pad was split, but the ash in the wound seemed to have stopped the bleeding.

"I'm sure that's sore, but I think you're going to live."

Chase had never owned a dog. His mother had been allergic to both cats and dogs. He'd always wanted a dog, but not under these circumstances. He got on the quad and put Pepe on his lap.

"Let's go see what's up the road."

A few minutes later, he saw two men. They had rags wrapped around their heads to keep the ash out. Chase slowed down so he wouldn't stir up too much ash. He stopped the quad about twenty feet away, removed his helmet and respirator, then walked up to them, carrying Pepe in the crook of his arm. When he reached them, Pepe started growling. The two men looked at the poodle as if they didn't know what it was. At first Chase thought they might be with the circus, but judging from Pepe's reaction, they couldn't be roustabouts. They'd know the dog, and Pepe would know them.

They must be from Lago. Chase smiled, wishing Cindy was with him so she could talk to them.

"*¿Hablas inglés?*"

The men shook their covered heads.

"I'm afraid that's about the extent of my Spanish," Chase said.

One of the men pointed at the quad.

"Yes." He turned his head to look at the quad. "I came up the road on —"

Chase's eyes rolled up in their sockets, he fell to his knees, and his world went from ash gray to pitch black.

03:33 PM

John pulled the truck onto the highway with a satisfied sigh.

"Not too bad," he said.

"Yeah," Mark said. "We only almost died twice."

"We'll go to the bridge. If we don't find them, we'll turn around and head back to Puebla. But first I'm going to rewrap the air filter."

This time Nicole and Mark got out with him to stretch their legs. Nicole wandered over to the edge of the road, carrying Chico. Suddenly, she screamed.

John and Mark ran over to them. At the bottom of the ravine was a stream. A smashed semitrailer marked with the Rossi Brothers' logo lay across it. Scattered around the trailer were four dead elephants.

Nicole had turned away from the terrible sight. "Rosy, Hannico, Me-Tu, and Hugo," she said quietly. "Hugo is . . . was . . . the father of Pet's calf."

Mark turned his camera away from the carnage as well, and put his arm around Nicole.

John was equally horrified, but he did not turn away. He looked up the road toward the bridge and saw where the shoulder must have broken off and fallen into the ravine. He ran back to the truck and grabbed his climbing rope and harness.

"What are you doing?" Nicole asked.

"I'm going down to check it out. How many people ride in the tractor?"

"Two. But there might be a third riding in the sleeper. Do you think they're still in there?"

"We'll see," John said, though from the look of the wreckage, he was certain no one had gotten out. The real question was, were they still alive? "What do your mom and sister drive?"

"They have a truck camper."

John was relieved to hear that. "Can you drive a quad?"

"Sure," Nicole said.

"I want you and Mark to head up to the bridge and see if anyone else has had an accident or is stranded." He pointed at the ravine. "The circus logo on the side of the trailer is pointing away from the bridge, which means they were heading to Puebla when they went off the road. They'd probably turned around when they saw the bridge was out."

"What made them go off the road?"

John pointed up the road. "Looks like they were in the right-hand lane coming around that curve. Maybe another quake. Or maybe the elephants got scared and rocked the trailer, and the drivers lost control. You can see where the pavement fell away. If you find something, let me know. If I find someone alive down there, I'll call you." He looked at Mark. "I need you to use your eyes without the camera."

"No problem," Mark said.

"Is your head okay?"

Mark smiled. "The only time you have to worry about my head, or any other part of my body, is when I'm not complaining."

John returned the smile. "That's what I figured." Back in his SEAL days, he'd had a team member just like Mark, a guy by the name of Raul Delgado. Raul used to constantly whine and complain, but when it was crunch time, he was the best operative they had. John had heard that Raul was now Commander Delgado, head honcho of SEAL Team One.

As Mark and Nicole off-loaded the quad, John rigged his ropes. It had been fifteen years since he had rappelled into a ravine, but he found his hands working the line and harness as if it were yesterday.

The only easy day was yesterday. Where had Chase heard that? It couldn't be a coincidence.

When he'd left the SEALs and married Emily, John Masters had put all that behind him. It wasn't until the lightning strike that it had all come back. He had even thought about reenlisting.

But where would that have left Chase?

Chase came to with a hammering headache, ash and bile in his mouth, and something tickling his face. His eyelids fluttered open. The thing tickling his face was Pepe's tongue. He didn't move as he tried to put together what had happened. He'd been talking to the two guys with the rags wrapped around their heads. One of them had pointed at the quad. Chase had turned to look and the lights had gone out.

He sat up very slowly, but not slowly enough. He threw up. He thought his head was going to explode. He felt the back of his skull and discovered a hard lump the size of a chicken egg.

He looked up the road. The quad was gone. He felt around his neck. The respirator was gone. So was his helmet and his go bag and . . . He felt his pockets. They were turned inside out. They had taken the sat phone and everything else.

In a disaster, desperate people do desperate things.

One of his father's warnings.

What was I supposed to do? Blow right by them without stopping?

He wished he had now.

Pepe barked.

He looked down at him. "Yeah, yeah, I know. You had them pegged. I should have listened to you."

Pepe barked again.

"I'm not picking you up. If I bend over, my head might roll off my neck."

Pepe did a backward flip.

"Nice trick. I'm still not picking you up."

Chase looked at his watch. He had been out cold for five minutes.

03:33 PM

John dropped over the edge as soon as Nicole and Mark took off on the quad. It was an easy rappel, but being among the broken elephants was much worse than seeing them from the road. Swarms of flies covered the carcasses, rising in a black mass as he made his way to the tractor. The respirator kept the dust out, but not the stench of rotting flesh.

He walked past the colorful trailer, which was now nothing more than a pile of twisted metal. The tractor was on its side several feet from the trailer. The fuel tank had ruptured, coating the tractor with slick diesel. One of the men had been ejected through the windshield and was lying twenty feet from the tractor. Two other men were seat-belted in the cab. Both were just as dead as the man on the ground.

He looked up at the road. He could see more clearly now how it had happened. A good portion of the outside lane had collapsed.

It must have happened at night, John thought. *They came around the corner, thinking the worst was over, then the world dropped out from under them.* Looking at the shattered bodies, he could not help but think of another accident on another mountain thousands of miles away. His wife and daughter, Emily and Monica, both killed on impact, while he had walked away without a cut or a bruise. Unscathed. Safe. Why? He shook the memory off, as he had so many times before. He was about to climb back up to the road, but a glint of metal farther off in the trees caught his attention. He reached it with some difficulty. It was a second semi, smaller than the elephant truck but equally destroyed. Two dead men crushed in the cab. It was impossible to get to, or even see into, the sleeper behind the men. He called out and listened. There was no reply.

He looked up at the road again. He could barely see it from this position, which is why they hadn't seen the second truck from the road. He walked over to what was left of the trailer to see what they had been hauling.

Cats.

The ground was littered with lions and tigers. Some were still in their cages. Others had been thrown out onto the ground. He counted seven lions and three tigers. All dead.

Heartbreaking.

He did a thorough search of the area to make sure he hadn't missed anything, but when he finished, something was still nagging at him. He returned to the cat trailer and counted again.

Seven lions. Three tigers.

He called Nicole to find out how many cats the show had. She didn't answer.

Probably can't hear above the noise of the quad.

He called Mark. Again no answer.

He counted the cats for the third time, then he counted the cages.

Ten cats. Eleven cages.

He called Nicole and Mark again, and again there was no answer.

He climbed back up to the road as fast as he could.

The tiger watched the man climb the rope. The man had climbed down the rope faster than he was going up. The tiger had seen this countless times before in the big tent, from the humans who swung and walked the rope in the air. This man was not like the ones in the big tent. He did not sparkle and glitter in the light. And he was a new man. The tiger had not seen him before. The tiger had thought about coming out of hiding as he watched the man wander among the dead, but had waited instead. Since the fall in the dark, everything was new. Nothing was as it had been. The ground had shaken. The sky rained dust. The tiger was afraid of this new world, but also intrigued by it. And hungry. He heard the truck door close and the engine rumble and the tires move along the pavement above. He waited until the sound faded away, then came out of hiding. He walked to the stream and drank. A movement to his right caught his attention. A deer bounding up the steep bank to the road. He knew deer, but not like this. At the farm during the long days of stillness with no man in the ring snapping the whip, making him do things, he was sometimes given deer to eat. But this deer was full of life. It moved with strength and grace up the mountain-side. The tiger was hungry. It followed the deer.

Nicole drove the quad slowly down the left lane of the highway, with Chico clinging to her front, and Mark clinging to her back.

"Not so close to the edge," Mark reminded her for the twentieth time. "I'm not wearing a helmet."

"A helmet won't do you much good if we plunge over the side."

"Thanks for reminding me. And that's exactly what I'm afraid of. Scoot over!"

"If I get too far over, we won't be able to see into the ravine."

"Then at least keep your eyes on the road. I'll watch the ravine and tell you if I see anything horrible."

It was hard for Nicole to imagine what could be more horrible than four dead elephants and a smashed circus truck. The image would be tattooed in her memory forever. If they hadn't stopped where they had, they probably would never have seen the elephant rig. She dreaded seeing her mother and sister's crushed camper, or any of the other circus rigs, but she felt compelled to keep peering over the edge. Chico had gotten away from the clown rig. Pepe had gotten away from the dog rig. She hoped they weren't the only survivors.

She eased the quad around a sharp curve and nearly fell off the seat. There were at least thirty cars, campers, and Rossi Brothers' Circus trailers blocking the highway. She throttled the quad to full speed and came to a sliding stop in the midst of the vehicles.

"Thanks for that experience," Mark said.

Nicole jumped off the quad and ran toward a tall, thin man wearing a red wig, oversize floppy shoes, and clown makeup.

"Doug!" she shouted.

"I can't believe this!" the clown shouted back. He threw his long arms around her and Chico, who seemed as happy to see Doug as Nicole was. "What are you doing here? How did you get here?"

A crowd gathered around them. Mark unwrapped the bungee cord securing his camera to the back of the quad and started videotaping.

"Where are my mom and sister?"

"Mexico City. I'm sure they're worried sick. . . ."

"They're not in Mexico City. We were just —"

"Maybe they got stuck at the village."

"What village?"

"The Lake of the Mountain. It's up near the rim of the volcano."

"Lago?"

"Yeah, I think they called it that. It's Arturo's village."

"Why would they go up there?"

"The orphanage. Your mom took the dog act, Chico, and a few clowns to . . . Wait — how did you get your hands on Chico?"

"This isn't getting us anywhere," Nicole interrupted. "You go first. From the beginning."

"All right." Doug took a deep breath. "The day before yesterday, a priest shows up at the matinee in Puebla with a half dozen kids from an orphanage. He could only bring a few of the kids because he doesn't have a way to transport them all." Doug smiled. "You know your mom, she's a sucker for kids. So she offers to do a free show for the orphanage. You know, a mini show. Some clowns. The dog act. Ponies for the kids to ride. The priest invites them to spend the night. Your mom and her crew take off for Lago halfway through the big show. She wants to get up to the village at a decent hour so they can get some sleep, get up early, and do the show. She wants to get over to Mexico City by early afternoon. The priest offers to lead them to Lago, which he says is kind of hard to find in the dark.

"We finish the last act, strike the big top, and decide to drive straight to Mexico City. Maybe get there at three in the morning and have a day off to do laundry, look around, you know . . . Anyway, we're driving down the highway in a caravan and everything's fine and then suddenly it feels like the world's coming apart. We pull over, wait it out, gather our wits, and take off again. We get maybe a quarter of a mile up the road and run into this gigantic landslide. We try to get ahold of your mom, but all the cells are dead. We turn around and come back here because it's a good place to pull the rigs off the road. The elephant guys decide to go back to Puebla.

Because we were heading straight to Mexico City, they hadn't bothered to load up with hay and grain. The cat guys decided to go with them. Don't ask me why. They leave with a promise to find out if there's another way to Mexico City. No point in all of us going to Puebla until we find out.

"By noon the next day, we still haven't heard from the elephant crew or the cat guys, so we send a car to Puebla to find out what's up. They don't get very far either. They run into a landslide bigger than the one in front of us. They drive back and tell us what's up. One of the tumblers crawls over the slide in front of us and finds out the bridge up ahead is out. We can't go forward. We can't go backward. We're stuck between a rock and a hard place. Then the ash starts coming down, so we set up tents to keep it off us and our new friends." He pointed to some of the people standing around. "Not everybody here's on the show. We took in the locals who got stranded with us. A couple of us are clowning to entertain the kids and keep the grown-ups' minds off the situation."

"I was wondering why you were clowning," Nicole said.

"The concession trucks are with us, so we have plenty of food. There's a stream down in the gully running along the road. We've been hauling water up, so we aren't going to die of thirst any time soon. I figure we can last a couple of weeks if we don't get sick of hot dogs before then."

"I wouldn't drink that water," John Masters said. No one had noticed him pull up.

Nicole looked at him with hopeful eyes.

John shook his head. "They didn't make it. How many cats does the show have?"

"Eleven," Doug answered. "Seven lions and four tigers."

"One of the tigers is missing," John said, then explained what he had found upstream.

04:06PM

"Stop!" Cindy shouted.

Tomás slammed on the brakes.

"There are no tire tracks in front of us," she said in Spanish.

Tomás looked through the windshield and nodded. He pointed at her sat phone.

Cindy looked down at the phone's screen. "No satellite signal."

Tomás put the truck into reverse and turned it around. A couple miles down the road, they found the disturbed ash. They got out for a closer look and found the tire tracks going back in the direction Chase had come from.

"Footprints," Tomás said.

"And animal prints," Cindy added.

"*Muy pequeño.*"

"Very small," Cindy agreed.

They got into the truck and followed the tracks all the way back to the slide. There was a man sitting on the rubble, wearing Chase's respirator and helmet. Sitting next to him was Chase's go bag. Tomás was out of the truck in a flash. The man got up and tried to run away but fell. Tomás yanked him to his feet, slapped the helmet off of his head, and tore the respirator off his face.

"I think his leg is broken!" Cindy shouted.

Tomás either didn't understand or didn't care. He dragged the blubbering man over to the edge of the road. The quad was smashed against a tree thirty feet below them. Lying next to it was another man.

"*¿Muerto?*" Tomás asked.

"*Sí*," the man said. He looked at Cindy. "My friend is dead."

"So you speak English," Cindy said with absolutely no sympathy for him. "Where is *our* friend?"

"We left the boy on the road."

"Alive?"

"Yes."

"He had better be."

Tomás marched the man to the truck and pushed him into the bed, ignoring his protests.

"We go," he told Cindy.

Cindy ran to the passenger door and jumped in. She was afraid that in his present mood, Tomás would leave her behind.

Tomás stepped on the gas, but they didn't get very far. A hundred yards down the road, the right front tire exploded.

Chase walked up the road in the direction of Lago with Pepe at his feet, stirring up tiny puffs of ash with each dainty step. He was no longer limping.

Where are Tomás and Cindy? What's taking them so long?

It had been over an hour since he had told them it was clear.

Maybe Tomás found a better way up and is in front of me. But where are the tire tracks?

The only tracks in front of him were the thieves' boot prints reminding him how stupid he'd been. The pounding in his head had diminished to a dull thud, but his anger had not. He came around yet another curve in the winding ash-covered road and stopped. In front of him was a crack in the earth that ran across the road and up the mountain as far as he could see. White steam billowed out of the crack. It was as if the ground had been unzipped, leaving a gap thirty feet across. In the middle of the gap were two upended trucks with the Rossi Brothers' Circus logo painted on their sides. One truck had a camper on the back. The other truck had been pulling a trailer, which was now a twisted wreck. Scattered around the smashed trailer were at least a dozen dog crates. The wire-mesh doors were all hanging open. Chase looked inside one of the crates and saw what looked like dried blood. There was a second trailer just off the road. Inside were four dead ponies.

Pepe barked.

"I hear you," Chase said. "You were lucky to get away with an injured paw." He looked at the trucks. The passenger's and driver's doors were open, just like the crates. "Looks like everyone got out." He scratched Pepe's ears. "This explains how you got up here, but it doesn't explain *why* you were up here, or where everyone went."

The trucks formed a bridge across the gap, which the circus people must have used to get to the other side.

And there's no doubt the thieves used the same bridge to get to my side, Chase thought. He was still angry, but looking at the steam coming out of the crack, he couldn't really blame them. The mountain was coming apart. The two men had been in a panic, with a long, dangerous walk ahead of them. He just wished they had left the go bag with the sat phone and his water. He was thirsty and he was sure the others were wondering why he hadn't checked in or answered the phone.

Chase looked down the road where he had come from. The curve was sharp. With the ash flying around, there was a good chance Tomás wouldn't see the crack before he crashed into it. Chase had to warn them. He thought about walking back and flagging them down. But what if they didn't drive up the road? What if something had happened to the truck? A flat tire, mechanical breakdown, getting mired in the soft ground . . . The possibilities were endless.

He looked up at the sky. It was getting darker, and it wasn't just the ash. The sun was getting lower. It would be pitch dark in a couple of hours. He couldn't wrap himself in toilet paper like they had the air filters. His eyes were swollen, his throat was sore. He needed water. He needed shelter. And he needed both of them soon.

You're no good to anybody if you're dead . . . including yourself.

Another of his father's favorite sayings. He wondered if that one was a Navy SEAL deal too. The SEAL motto Cindy had told him about was certainly holding up. The only easy day *was* yesterday. The hardest thing they'd done the day before was move a lion and slap a bear on the butt, and it was Momma Rossi who had slapped the bear.

"Guess I better get my own butt in gear," Chase said.

Pepe barked and ran into one of the crates.

"I'm not carrying you in one of those, but I will carry you across the junkyard bridge so you don't fall into the steaming crevasse." He squatted down. "Let's go."

Pepe gave him another bark, but didn't budge.

Chase got an idea. He reached into the crate and pulled Pepe out.

"I need this."

He picked up Pepe's crate and a couple others, then jogged back down to the spot where the curve straightened out. It was roughly thirty yards from the crack. He came back and picked up a few more crates, then returned for a third and fourth load.

"Fifteen crates," he said. "We're going to build a pyramid."

Chase set out five crates in the middle of the road, then four on top of the five, then three on top of the four, then two on top of the three, topping it off with Pepe's crate, which was the smallest.

Pepe did a backflip and landed on the first tier.

"Nice," Chase said. "But this isn't a circus prop. It's a stop sign. The truck will have to slow down as it's coming around the curve. Tomás will stop when he sees the crates, or he'll run into them. Either way, he won't fall through the crack."

Pepe stared at him.

"I can't believe I'm explaining this to a poodle."

He picked Pepe up and started toward the crack in the earth.

04:21PM

"I'm sorry about your friends," Mark said.

"Thanks," Doug said. "I guess this is the end of the Rossi Brothers' Circus. No cat act. No elephant act." He looked off into the distance. "Maybe no owner. We all knew it was coming, but we had no idea it was going to end this way."

Doug was smiling, but it was clear from his voice and the expression beneath the greasepaint that he was anything but happy. When he'd heard about the elephants and cats and his friends, he had nearly collapsed. John and Mark had to help him into the tent where he could sit down.

John was out trying to make a phone call, Nicole was in the opposite corner of the tent talking quietly to the other circus people, leaving Mark to look after the bereaved clown. He didn't mind. He liked clowns.

"What's the deal with the camera?" Doug asked.

Mark explained the last forty-eight hours as best as he could.

"The Rossis lost their house!" Doug said. "We didn't even hear about the hurricane. Does Mrs. Rossi know?"

"I don't think so. We haven't been able to get in touch with anyone down here to let them know."

"You're making a documentary about this John dude?"

"I'm just the camera guy. My producer, Cindy, is making the documentary. But it's a safe bet you'll be in it."

"Clown on a volcano," Doug said.

Mark smiled. "Something like that."

"Might be my last performance."

John came into the tent, looking worried. Nicole saw him enter and ran over to join Mark and Doug as he walked up to them.

"I spoke to Cindy, but the conversation was garbled. The ash is playing havoc with the satellite signal. She said she completely lost the signal for a while. From what I understood, a couple of men jacked Chase's quad and he's missing. Tomás found the thieves. They had totaled the quad, and one of them is dead. The other guy has a broken leg. To top it off, Tomás had a blowout, which caused some other damage to the truck besides the flat. Cindy's walking ahead trying to find Chase while Tomás tries to fix the truck. It sounds like the ash is a lot worse up there than it is down here."

"What do we do?" Nicole asked.

"*We* do nothing," John said. "You and Mark are going to stay here. I'm going back up to find Chase."

"I'm going with you," Nicole said.

John shook his head. "You'll be safer here. I'm not going back the same way we came. That would take too long. I've figured out a way of going over the top. Or close to the top.

I'll get the truck up as far as I can, then head out on foot or on the quad to Lago. There's only one road going in. If I get there before Tomás and Cindy, I'll backtrack along the road."

"I'm still going with you," Nicole said.

"Sorry," John said.

"My mother and sister are in Lago. It's the reason I came all the way down here."

"It's why Cindy and I came down here too," Mark said. "Who's to say it's any safer here than it is up at the village? Stranded is stranded."

"Are you saying that you want to go too?" John asked.

"Not particularly, but Cindy would probably kill me if I didn't." Mark smiled. "Besides, you're lucky. Bad things happen all around you, but you always come through without a scratch. You're the Teflon man. Nothing seems to stick to you, so I'm sticking *with* you."

"You're forgetting that if we have to use the quad, there's only room for two people," John said.

"If it comes to that, I'll flip you for it," Mark said.

"What about my luck?"

"I'll take my chances."

"What about us?" Doug asked.

"I spoke to the authorities in Mexico City. They know you're stranded here. There's a road crew on the way to repair the bridge and clear the slide."

"How long is that going to take?" Doug asked.

"Too long," John admitted. "But I think I have that covered as well. A friend of mine in the States is trying to get permission to bring a rescue team in with choppers. As soon as they get the okay, they'll mobilize quickly. It won't take them more than a few hours to get here."

"How'd you arrange that?"

"My friend is in charge of the outfit."

"A military outfit?" Nicole asked.

"Definitely military." John looked at Doug. "The best thing you can do while you're waiting is to set up a landing zone. You'll have to move some of these trucks. They'll fly in and ferry you to the other side of the bridge, where you'll be driven to Mexico City."

"What about the animals?" Doug asked.

"That's up to Delgado."

"Delgado?" Mark asked.

"Commander Raul Delgado of the U.S. Navy SEALs." John smiled. "He reminds me of you, actually. Constantly whining and complaining, but he's the best operative I know. His priority is going to be getting the people out of here, not the animals, but you never know with Raul. He's done some crazy things in his life. He might like the idea of evacuating lions and tigers and bears." John looked at Nicole and Mark. "Time to go."

It was time for Chase to go. He put the dusty poodle down his shirt and started across the junkyard bridge. The short crossing turned out to be a lot harder than he was expecting. The wrecks were hot with steam and slick with ash. And

Pepe's sharp nails scratching his stomach and chest as the little dog tried to get out wasn't helping matters.

"Knock it off! Unless you want to fall off into the bottomless pit."

Chase knew it wasn't bottomless, but it was deep. He couldn't see the bottom. He got down on his hands and knees, afraid he would slip off if he stayed on his feet. As he crawled onto the camper roof, the pile suddenly shifted with a loud screech. He froze and held his breath.

This is it.

The screeching stopped. The twisted metal held. Chase breathed.

Forward or backward?

He looked behind him. The distance was just about equal.

Dead center.

He didn't like the sound of that.

In the middle. Halfway. Better.

Pepe had stopped struggling. It was as if he sensed the danger. Whatever the reason, Chase was grateful. It would make his next move easier.

Whatever that move is going to be.

There wasn't enough room to turn around safely. He'd have to crawl backward to get to where he'd come from. The other problem was that when the camper shifted, the top had settled at a steep angle. He was hanging on to the edge to keep himself from slipping into the crack.

"Just go!" he shouted.

He crawled forward, feeling the pile tremble every time he put a hand or a knee down. The far side seemed like it was a football field away.

If there's another earthquake . . . If the crack widens . . . If I slip . . .

Chase knew better than to think this way. *Fear brings disaster from the inside out.* His father had told him this a thousand times. *Focus on the moment. Concentrate on survival. Think about what's right, not what's wrong. Take advantage of it.*

Chase wished his father was there to explain what was "right" about this. After what seemed like an eternity, he finally reached the other side of the junkyard bridge, but he was far from safe. The edge of the road was several feet above him. He would have to stand on the tilted truck hood, reach above his head, and pull himself up. He got to his feet very slowly, looking for something solid to grab on to if the pile started to go. The camper rocked back and forth. Pepe began struggling again.

"Can't have that."

He reached into his shirt and pulled him out.

"Sorry."

He tossed the poodle up over the ledge. Pepe landed with a soft thud and a whimper. A second later, his head appeared over the edge and he started barking indignantly.

"No need to thank me," Chase said.

He reached up and grabbed the overhang of broken road. Pepe licked his fingers.

"That's not helpful."

He pulled himself up, relieved to have his feet off the unstable camper, and even happier to have climbed onto the road. He lay on his back, catching his breath, with Pepe perched on his chest.

04:47 PM

Tomás pulled the truck over and Cindy got in. She told him about her broken conversation with John Masters. Tomás told her about the conversation he'd had with the broken-legged thief in back while changing the tire and repairing the undercarriage.

The man had said that he and his friend were working in Lago when the earthquake hit in the middle of the night. There had been a great deal of damage to the houses, and people had been killed, but he didn't know how many or who.

Cindy looked at Tomás's children smiling in the photos taped to the dash. Tomás wasn't showing it, but she was certain he was sick with worry.

Tomás explained that the village priest had returned to Lago just after the earthquake with a van full of orphans, three circus clowns, a dozen performing dogs, and two very small women.

"Mrs. Rossi and Nicole's sister, Leah," Cindy said.

Tomás nodded.

Mrs. Rossi, Leah, and two of the clowns had been badly injured. A few miles from Lago the road had opened up, swallowing the Rossis' camper and the other vehicle. The priest and orphans had been right in front of them and had missed falling into the enormous crack by inches. Because that road was the only way in or out, Lago was completely cut off. The two men had decided to head out on foot. They were both from Puebla and wanted to find out how their families were. They were surprised to see Chase drive up on the quad. The man with the broken leg claimed he had no idea that his friend was going to hit Chase in the head and take the quad.

"Do you believe him?" Cindy asked.

Tomás shrugged.

Neither of the men had ever driven a quad. When they reached the landslide, his friend took the quad off-road and it flipped. The man in back crawled up the bank because he didn't know what else to do. He had been expecting to die there.

"He may yet die," Tomás concluded in English, "if Chase is unwell."

Cindy took her phone out, hoping to reach Nicole with the news about her mother and sister. The signal was gone again.

John drove the truck up the mountainside at an impossible angle.

Mark was holding on to his precious camera with white knuckles. "You know," he said, "these tires don't have suction cups."

"But we do have a roll bar," John said. "If we flip, we should be okay."

"Comforting," Mark said.

"Do we have a signal yet?" John asked.

Nicole tore her eyes away from the tops of the trees and glanced at the satellite phone she was carrying. "No."

"Maybe it will get better when we get above the tree line."

"*If* we get to the tree line," Mark said. "Where did you learn to drive?"

"In the Navy."

"Figures."

"Lago de la Montaña," Chase said. Pepe looked up at him. "I'm not sure how you say it in poodle, but in English it means 'Lake of the Mountain.'"

The last half mile of road had been steep. The small lake was above the tree line and fed by glaciers, which had now turned from white to gray. The village was on the opposite side of the lake. Looming behind it like a petrified tooth was the summit of Popocatepetl. A thick plume of gray ash and steam billowed from the peak into the darkening sky as far as Chase could see.

Pepe scampered to the edge of the water and started drinking. Chase joined him. The surface was covered with fine ash and what looked like white floating rocks. He picked one up. It was porous and as light as a feather.

"Pumice stone," he said.

Pepe picked one up in his teeth and tossed it into the air.

"Knock yourself out. It's not poisonous."

Chase kneeled, cleared an area of ash and pumice, and scooped water into his mouth. He wasn't aware of just how thirsty he was until the icy liquid hit the back of his throat. He put his head under water and came up gasping from the glacial chill.

"Whoa!"

Having his face clean made every other part of his body itch. He looked across the lake at the village. It had taken him so long to get this far, five minutes more couldn't hurt. He quickly stripped off his clothes, tossed them into the water to soak, then dove in. He thought his heart would turn to ice. He lifted his head above the water. His teeth chattered. Pumice stones bobbed around him like an armada of toy ships. Pepe ran back and forth along the shore, barking.

"Come on in! The water's fine!"

Pepe would have none of it. Chase stayed in as long as he could, which was less than three minutes. He waded back to shore, shivering. Facing the lake, he rinsed and wrung out his clothes as the air dried his skin. The wind had died down to almost nothing, which meant the ash was not blowing around as much, for which he was grateful. It meant he might be reasonably clean when he got to Lago. As he pulled on his underwear, he heard something behind him. He turned, expecting to see Pepe tossing more pumice around. Pepe was there, but he wasn't tossing volcanic rock, and he wasn't alone. He was sitting next to an old man and five children. Next to the old man was a wheelbarrow filled with sticks. The five children were carrying bundles of sticks in their arms and giggling. He didn't blame them. A second earlier, they had been staring at his shivering butt. He would have laughed too.

He quickly pulled on the rest of his clothes.

When he was dressed, the old man said something to him, which Chase didn't understand.

"*No hablo español. ¿Hablas inglés?*"

The old man shook his head.

Chase pointed at the village. "Lago de la Montaña?"

The old man nodded.

That was just about the extent of Chase's Spanish. He thought about mentioning Tomás's name, but realized he didn't know Tomás's last name.

I've known Tomás my entire life. How could I not know his last name? He looked at the five children. He did know what Tomás's children looked like, though, and none of them were here with the old man.

Why are children out gathering wood?

He would have to *see* why when he got to Lago because he didn't know how to ask.

Tomás eased around the curve, then stepped on the gas. He didn't see the dog crates until they were bouncing off the windshield. He slammed on the brakes.

"What was that?" Cindy shouted.

Tomás shook his head.

They got out. The man in the truck bed moaned. Tomás checked on him before coming around to the front of the truck, where Cindy was pulling something out from under the bumper.

"Dog crates. Obviously from the circus, but why did they leave them in the middle of the road? And where are the dogs?"

Tomás squatted down and looked at the ground in front of the truck.

"What do you see?"

"Footprints."

They followed them to the crack.

"Chase put the crates there to warn us," Cindy said.

Tomás got down on his knees and pushed on the trailer to test its stability. It moved. He took the flashlight from his go bag and leaned over the edge with it. Cindy had seen him and John do the same thing on the levee road during the worst of Hurricane Emily.

After a couple of minutes, Tomás popped back up and said, "I will go first."

This implied that Cindy was going second. She wasn't sure she wanted to go at all. "What about our friend in the truck?"

"He will have to stay here."

"Maybe I should stay with him."

Tomás shrugged and jogged back to the truck. He drove forward and parked it as far to the right side of the road as he could. He came back with a coil of rope and Chase's go bag slung over his shoulder. He tied one end of the rope to the bumper.

"What are you doing?" Cindy asked.

Instead of answering, he handed her a webbed harness with a carabiner attached to it.

"What am I supposed to do with this?"

Without a moment's hesitation, Tomás danced nimbly across the wreckage to the other side of the crack. The trailer and camper were still wobbling and screeching as he pulled himself up to the road.

"Are you with the circus?" Cindy shouted across the fissure. "I can't do that!"

Tomás wrapped the rope around a tree, took up the slack, and tied it off. He motioned for her to put the harness around her waist and clip the carabiner to the rope.

"You are crazy!"

Tomás pointed at his watch.

"I know you're in a hurry, but still . . . I can't do this. I'll stay here and take care of the man in the truck."

Tomás gave her another shrug and turned to leave.

"Wait!"

Tomás turned back.

Cindy snapped the carabiner to the rope. "Just go before you regain your sanity," she muttered to herself. She stepped onto the twisted metal and immediately dropped to her hands and knees. There was no way she'd be able to cross it like Tomás had. She began to crawl. Three quarters of the way across, she heard a loud rumbling coming up from the fissure. The wreckage started to sway. She looked up. The sides of the fissure were grinding back and forth like jaws. The metal dropped away as if the earth were swallowing it.

Cindy screamed.

05:16 PM

The old man was kneeling, with his arms wrapped around three of the children. Chase was crouched down, his arms around the other two and the poodle. Pepe was whimpering. The children were crying. As the ground rumbled and rolled beneath them, Chase looked up at the volcano. The plume had turned darker and thicker, as if someone were stoking the fire beneath. A church bell rang from the village. He wondered if someone was pulling the rope or if the quake was causing it to toll.

Chase had glanced at his watch the moment they had dropped to their knees in the middle of the road. When the quake finally stopped, only thirteen seconds had passed.

The shaking terrified the tiger. He unsheathed his claws and gripped the dirt so the ground would not drop out from beneath him. When it finally stopped, he continued to hold on for several seconds. He had lost track of the deer some time ago. Other scents were now pushing up the mountain. He lifted his head and listened. He heard the bang of metal in the trees below. He did not like the sound. It reminded him of the night before, when the world came apart and the other cats lay still. He moved away from the noise so it could not catch him.

John, Nicole, and Mark were sitting upside down, pushing airbags out of their faces. Thirteen seconds earlier, they had been heading up the mountain on a steep incline. The trees had begun to thin out, making it easier for John to pick and choose his route. The truck had started to slip sideways and tip to the left. John shouted for them to lean to the right, but their weight wasn't enough to put the truck back on four wheels. The 4x4 rolled over in slow motion and landed on its roof. Then it started to slide, spinning like a windmill, banging off several trees before coming to a jarring stop against a boulder.

"Everyone okay?" John asked.

"I'm fine," Nicole said.

"It seems to me that we were in this exact same position a couple of days ago," Mark said.

"Not the exact same position," John said. "That time we were on our side."

"Oh, yeah, that's right. On a train trestle!"

"Are you okay?" John repeated.

"Couldn't be better," Mark said. "Can we do that again?"

John unhooked his seat belt, righted himself, and kicked out the windshield. The three crawled out of the truck and looked it over. The quad had been smashed into several pieces.

"Guess we won't have to flip a coin to see who rides," Mark said.

John didn't hear him. He was already headed up the mountain.

Cindy dangled over the steaming chasm, suspended by her waist. Eternal blackness loomed beneath her. There was no sign of the wreckage she'd been crawling on a moment before. The earth had swallowed it. She reached up and grabbed the rope, not trusting the harness alone to hold her. The rope bowed under her weight. She was ten feet below the road's jagged edge. Was Tomás okay? Would the rope hold? Did she have the strength to pull herself up if it did?

Tomás's respirator-covered face appeared over the edge. He shined his flashlight down on her. Cindy could see only his eyes, but he looked as relieved to see her as she was to see him.

"Rope fraying. Stay still. I pull you up."

His face disappeared before she could ask him to explain.

Fraying *is not a word you want to hear when you're hanging from a rope*, Cindy thought, tightening her grip. As a television reporter, she had been in a lot of frightening situations, including Hurricane Emily, but this was by far the most terrified she had ever been. Her heart slammed in her chest. Tears poured from her eyes. She couldn't breathe. She tore the respirator off and dropped it into the void. She took a deep breath and started to choke. Something bad was in the air. *Sulfur? What's taking Tomás so long?* The end of a rope dropped down. She looked up.

"Tie to harness," Tomás shouted through his respirator. "Tight."

She fumbled with the line.

"Hurry!"

Cindy was doing the best she could. The respirator had not worked well against the foul air, but she realized now that it had been better than nothing. *What was I thinking? I've got to get out of this hole!* With fumbling fingers she managed to get the line through the carabiner and tie it off.

"Secured!" she shouted.

She began to pull herself along the rope, but found that Tomás was pulling her faster than she could move her hands. Within seconds he had her over the ledge and onto the road. He dragged her away from the crack and gave her a bottle of water. Her mouth and throat were raw from breathing ash and toxic steam, but she washed her face and rinsed her eyes before taking a drink.

"The village is not too far." Tomás helped her to her feet. He took his respirator off and handed it to her.

Cindy shook her head. "You keep it."

"Please. I insist."

Reluctantly, she put it on. Tomás took his shirt off, wet it down, and wrapped it around his nose and mouth.

They continued up the road toward Lago.

06:01PM

Brittle pumice popped beneath Chase's feet as he walked down the center of the road toward Lago. He had taken the bundles of sticks from the three smallest children. They in turn had taken Pepe and were handing him back and forth as they walked. As they drew closer to the village, they passed piles of rubble beside the road. At first Chase thought the piles were discarded building material or village garbage. But when the old man and the children stopped at one of the piles, crossed themselves, and bowed their heads, he knew he was wrong. The piles had once been houses. People had died beneath the debris. The group stopped three more times before entering the village.

Lago de la Montaña was much bigger than Chase had expected, and the damage also was much worse. The cobbled streets had buckled. The houses and buildings on both sides had all collapsed. The village was in ruins. The initial earthquake had struck at night while people were sleeping. Chase looked in dismay at the mounds of adobe brick and wood, knowing that some of the people, if not most of them, had died in their beds.

They arrived at the village square. It looked like a refugee camp, with dozens of people cooking, cleaning, and hovering outside crudely constructed shelters. The old man pointed at the church.

"Padre," he said. "Inside."

One wall of the church had collapsed, but the roof was intact. Popocatepetl's plume rose high above the steeple. The church's front door was open, and people were sitting on the stairs with blank, exhausted expressions. No one seemed even remotely interested in Chase's sudden appearance in the village.

Hopelessness. Defeat. He thought he had seen the look before in emergency shelters and on the faces of people standing outside what were once their homes, but this was different.

These people have given up. They are waiting for doom.

Two men came out of the church, carrying between them a body wrapped in a blanket. Everyone followed their progress across the square to the right of the church with dull eyes. The men lay the body on the ground among dozens of others.

The old man said something to the children. The one carrying Pepe handed him to Chase. Then they started distributing the sticks to the shelters for the pitiful fires.

Chase set Pepe on the ground. They had come to Lago to find Tomás's children, but he didn't know exactly where to start. Pepe decided for him. The little dog ran up the steps through the open doors of the church. Chase ran after him.

Dull light filtered through the cut-glass windows and the collapsed wall. Candles and oil lamps were scattered along the floor. Dark shadows flickered throughout the nave. It took a few seconds for Chase's eyes to adjust to the dark. The pews had been rearranged and turned into hospital beds. All of them were full. A murmuring of pain filled the church. Above the pitiful sound, Chase heard a high-pitched barking up near the altar. He wasn't sure why — Pepe wasn't his dog — but he felt responsible. He started to weave his way through the pews toward the front. It was a sad sight. The people lying on the makeshift beds were badly broken. Those who weren't hurt were helping those who were. Chase couldn't say it was exactly cheerful inside the church, but the mood was certainly more hopeful than it had been out on the square.

When Chase was halfway across the church, a man stepped out in front of him. He was wearing a black cassock dusted with ash, and a white clerical collar.

"Padre," Chase said.

"Yes. Are you with the circus?"

Chase shook his head, relieved to hear that the father spoke English. "My name is Chase Masters."

"I'm Father Alejandro, but you may call me Father Al, or just Al, if you like."

"I think I'll stick with Father Al," Chase said.

Father Al smiled. "And you say you are not with the circus."

"No, I just got here."

"The road is clear?" Father Al asked excitedly.

"No . . . sorry." Chase explained how he had gotten to the village and why he had come.

"I'm sorry about the men who robbed you. I know who they are, but they are not from here. They came from Puebla a few days ago to work in our bottling plant."

"Bottling plant?"

"*Agua* . . . water. The lake is glacial. Very pure. Montaña water is sold all over Mexico. Our other industry comes from the volcano itself. Perhaps you saw some of our product as you walked here."

"Pumice stone?"

"Yes. Plentiful." His expression turned serious. "Of course after this, I don't know what we will do. The village is in ruins. Many people have died. Others have left."

"Where did they go?" Chase asked. "How did they leave?"

"On foot in the middle of the night after the big earthquake. You climbed across the wreckage?"

"Yes."

"It is stable?"

"No. They couldn't have gone that way, and I didn't see anyone on the road coming up here besides those two men."

"I hope they are safe. You say you are here to check on a family?"

"The family of my father's partner, our friend. He's somewhere behind me. I'm sure he'll be here soon. His name is Tomás."

"That is a very common name. What is his last name?"

Chase flushed. "I don't know, but he's married to a woman named Guadalupe and they have eight children."

Father Al laughed. "That would be Tomás Vargas! The eight are not exactly his children, and Guadalupe is not exactly his wife. You say he's on his way up here?"

"I expect him any time," Chase said, hoping that nothing had happened to Tomás and Cindy.

Father Al gave him a broad smile. "That is wonderful news! Tomás has very clever hands. The generator is out. It is our only source of electricity. We tried to fix it but failed."

Tomás does have clever hands, Chase thought. *If anyone can fix the generator, Tomás can.*

"What do you mean, the children aren't exactly his children?" Chase asked.

"Yes," Father Al said, "I should explain. The eight children are orphans. Tomás pays all of their expenses, including their education if they decide to go to the university. Guadalupe runs the orphanage for the church. She and Tomás have been friends since they were children. They were both raised in the orphanage."

Chase had known none of this, but he wasn't completely surprised by the revelation. Tomás was a man of few words. It was probably just simpler for him to say that they were his kids and Guadalupe was his wife. It made no difference. He obviously loved them or he wouldn't be down here. Neither would Chase's father.

"Are the kids okay?"

"Oh, yes. We lost no one in the orphanage. In fact, two of those children were with me at the circus in Puebla. The orphanage is behind the church. It's the only building in Lago with virtually no damage."

"Then all the houses have been searched?"

"Yes. We started right after the big earthquake. Most of the people here were pulled from the rubble of their homes. Many of the people in the square have been up for two days straight looking for survivors. They are exhausted. I called the search off just two hours ago so they can get some rest. We will resume the search tomorrow when it's light, although I fear we've found all we are going to find." Father Al sighed. "Alive, anyway.

"The mother and daughter who run the circus are badly injured, I'm afraid. They are in the orphanage, where we set up our first hospital. As you can see, it has overflowed here, into the church. The three clowns and the dog trainer who came with them are bruised but fine."

"The Rossis are here?"

"So you know them. Leah and her mother."

"That was their camper?" Chase said.

"Unfortunately, yes."

"I've — we've been looking for them, too. The people I was traveling with before, I mean. I knew those vehicles belonged to the circus. I just didn't know who was driving them." Chase was shocked. He wondered if his father had heard about this, or Nicole.

"The uninjured circus people are outside the orphanage, resting. Like the villagers in the square, they have been up for two days searching for survivors."

"The orphanage . . ." Chase said slowly. "I walked into the village with an older man and five children. Were they from the orphanage?"

"Gathering wood?"

Chase nodded.

Father Al smiled. "We have been giving the children small jobs like gathering firewood to keep their minds off the tragedy and the volcano."

"What about the volcano?" Chase asked.

Father Al shrugged. "I have lived in Popocatepetl's shadow for over thirty years. This is the worst of the eruptions and it might be the end of Lago de la Montaña, but there is nothing we can do. The injured are not strong enough to walk off this mountain, and they outnumber those who are well, so we cannot carry them. It is up to God."

Chase understood Father Al's reasoning, but he had been taught his entire life that there is always something you can do. "So you're saying it's fate," he said.

Father Al shook his head. "Not fate. *Faith.* Come with me. I will take you to see the Rossis."

07:05 PM

John, Nicole, and Mark stepped above the tree line just after sunset. In front of them, Popocatepetl's plume shot up into the night sky, thousands of feet above the summit.

"It looks close enough to touch," Nicole said with awe.

"It's farther away than you think," John said. "It just looks close because of its size."

Mark started videotaping.

"It would be a lot easier for you if you weren't lugging that camera," John said.

"Do you see all the colors in the plume?" Mark asked, totally ignoring the suggestion. "We couldn't see them during the day, but at night it's like the Fourth of July."

"Lightning," Nicole said.

"I see it," John said.

Crackling white and gold bolts exploded through the plume like electrified spiderwebs.

"Does lightning make you nervous?" Mark asked.

John stared at the powerful column, remembering what Momma Rossi had said. *That lightning is still looking for you. . . . It's going to find you again. . . .* Reflexively, his hand went up to his earring.

"It *should* make me nervous," he admitted. "But for some reason, it doesn't." Then he pulled his sat phone out as he said abruptly to Mark and Nicole, "Get your headlamps out of your go bags. We'll need them to see where we're heading."

He tried the phone. Still no signal.

Tomás and Cindy had their headlamps on. They had reached the lake and were drinking the cold water and washing the ash from their faces and hair.

"I'm worried about that plume," Cindy said in Spanish.

"The pressure is being relieved," Tomás replied in his native tongue. "It is good."

"What about the lava?"

"There will be lava on the summit, but it is not a problem. It moves very slowly and hardens before it can reach Lago. Mudflows from melting snow and ice, earthquakes, and flying rocks are what we have to worry about. When I was young, a rock the size of a school bus fell on the village square. It was on a Sunday morning. Everyone was in church. No one died."

Cindy pointed across the lake. "Are those fires?"

Tomás nodded. "Campfires in the village square. It means people no longer have houses to return to. We should go."

Chase stood beside two small beds in the orphanage. They were children's beds, but the adults occupying them did not fill their length. On his left was Mrs. Rossi. On his right was Nicole's sister, Leah. Mrs. Rossi was unconscious. Leah was asleep. The village doctor had been tending to them when Father Al showed Chase into the girls' dormitory. The doctor finished his work, then turned to Chase and explained the extent of their injuries in English almost as good as Father Al's.

"Both women have broken ribs and severe concussions. Mrs. Rossi has two broken wrists and there is some damage to her neck, but without an X-ray machine or CAT scanner here, I can't say how bad the injuries are. I have stabilized the women, but they need to be hospitalized. I have sedated Mrs. Rossi, and of course they are both on pain medication." He looked at Father Al. "How are the patients in the church?"

"We lost Mrs. Ruiz," Father Al answered sadly.

The doctor nodded. "The medical supplies?"

"Very low. We are down to the expired medications. We are boiling cloth in the square to make dressings."

The doctor looked at his watch. "I'd better check on the other patients."

"And I need to see how the food supplies are holding up in the square," Father Al said.

"I'll stay here," Chase volunteered.

"One of the circus people is over in that corner, sleeping," Father Al said, nodding toward the man.

Chase looked over. He hadn't noticed the man sprawled on the tiny bed in the dark corner, with his knees hanging over the end.

"I believe his name is Dennis," Father Al continued. "He's one of the circus clowns. They took turns caring for the Rossis while the others helped us search the rubble for survivors. The dog trainer even enlisted some of the poodles to help. The little dogs found three people we would have missed otherwise."

The poodles were being kept in a large pen on the orphanage playground. The circus people had been asleep when Chase tiptoed up to put Pepe in the pen with his friends. He thought the little dog might start barking and wake everyone, but Pepe trotted over to the pile of his fellow poodles sleeping in the corner and snuggled into them without a whimper.

"If there are any problems, I'll be in the church," the doctor said. "When the girl wakes up, she will be thirsty. You can give her water but not too much. There is a case of Montaña under the bed. It's also important that she and her mother do not move. I've only been able to splint and wrap the broken bones. Undue movement could cause further damage. In fact . . ." He reached into his pocket and took out some pills. "If the girl wakes up, give her two of these."

"What are they?"

"They're sedatives, but tell her they're antibiotics. She's been a little difficult. Hard to keep down. I was thankful when she finally fell asleep. The best thing for her now is to rest."

07:26 PM

John stopped and pulled the topo map out of his go bag.

"Are we lost?" Mark asked.

"Not exactly," John answered. "I just need to check on where we're going."

"What about the GPS?" Nicole asked.

"You need a satellite signal to use the GPS." John pulled out a compass.

"We *are* lost," Mark said.

"Not as long as we keep the plume on our right. We're about here." He pointed to a spot on the map. "Here's the lake and the village." He moved his finger. "They're above the tree line, so we should be able to see them from this vantage point if they have any lights on."

"If they have electricity," Mark said.

John nodded. "That's the tricky part. If the power's out, Lago is going to be hard to spot, especially with all this ash floating around. They'll be using candles and lamps and have fires going in their houses. It's warm up here because of the plume, but down in the village, I'm betting it gets pretty cold when the sun goes down. I realize the plume is entertaining with the colors and lightning, but we're going to have to concentrate our attention down the mountain to the left. If we miss Lago, we could end up circling the mountain clockwise. I'd prefer not to do that if possible."

"Circling the drain," Mark said.

John laughed. "I haven't heard that phrase in years. And you're right. If we miss the village, we'll be in big trouble."

They started off again, looking down the mountain rather than up at the plume. John took the lead, followed by Mark, then Nicole.

Being a competitive swimmer, Nicole had great stamina, but she was learning that walking sideways on a volcano was using muscles she didn't know she had. Her legs and joints were killing her. But what bothered her more than her aching muscles was that skinny Mark, who looked like he'd never seen the inside of a gym, was loping behind John Masters with the ease of a mountain goat. And what about John Masters? She wouldn't be surprised to see him start flying. All he seemed to need was a sip of water and something to do, and he was good to go. Seemingly forever.

She was still terribly worried about her mother and Leah. . . . *And now Chase*, she thought. *I can't believe he got robbed in this desolate place. I just hope Tomás and Cindy have caught up to him and that he's okay. What if he's alone in the dark, maybe injured, maybe even —*

She stopped suddenly, then took a step backward and shined her headlamp down to make sure, hoping her eyes had been playing tricks on her in the dark. They weren't.

"Back here," she called out.

John and Mark were about thirty feet ahead of her. Their headlamps turned in her direction.

"What is it?" John asked.

"Don't tell me you've found another chimp," Mark said.

"You'd better come look."

The men walked back to where she was standing. She hadn't moved an inch.

"Well?" John said.

Nicole shined her headlamp down. "On the ground."

"My God!" Mark said. "They have bears here?"

"That's not a bear track," Nicole said, her mouth suddenly dry. "It's a tiger track."

07:45PM

Chase sat between Mrs. Rossi's and Leah's beds, trying hard to stay awake. The last patient he had watched like this was his father. The doctor and nurses had begged him to go home, but he had stubbornly refused. The only time he'd left his father's hospital bed was to go to the bathroom. He'd even eaten his food in the chair next to the bed, willing his father to come out of his coma.

Mrs. Rossi and Leah were pretty, like Nicole. The same black hair. The same complexion. With their eyes closed, he could only guess at the color, but he bet they were brown. Except for their height, it was obvious they were all related.

Leah began to stir. Her eyes fluttered open.

He smiled. *Brown.*

"Who are you?" Leah asked.

The blunt question startled him. He should have been thinking about what he was going to say in the event that she woke up.

"My name is Chase Masters."

"You're American."

"Yeah."

"What are you doing down here?"

"I'm a friend of Nicole's."

"My sister, Nicole?" She started to sit up and winced in pain.

"You'd better stay down."

"Okay. Is there any water?"

Chase took a bottle of Montaña water out of the case beneath the bed. As he unscrewed the cap, he looked at the colorful label. It featured the lake, the church, and, looming behind them, an erupting Popocatepetl. He gave Leah a sip.

"That's better," she said.

"Oh . . . the doctor wanted you to take these." He handed her the two pills.

"What are they?"

"Antibiotics." He was off to a great start with Nicole's sister. He told himself that it was for her own good, but that didn't make him feel better about lying to her.

She popped the pills into her mouth and washed them down.

"You say you're a friend of my sister's?"

"We came down to look for you after we heard about the earthquake."

Leah's eyes went wide. "Nicole's here?"

"Not here, but she's . . . uh . . . close." Chase had no idea where Nicole was. If they hadn't heard about the Rossis being in Lago, they were probably in Puebla by now.

"I must be dreaming," Leah said.

Chase tried to explain, but it was difficult because he didn't want to tell her about the hurricane and losing her home. She had enough to worry about. When he finished his abridged story, she asked for another drink of water and seemed to be thinking about what he had told her. She turned her head and looked at her mother.

"How is she?"

"She's . . . uh . . . sedated."

Leah nodded. "We need to get her to a hospital. What are the chances of us getting out of here?"

"Not real good at the moment. There's only one road in and it's impassable."

"Then how did you get here?"

"I climbed over the trucks jammed in the gap. I wouldn't want to do that again."

"I bet. So your friend Tomás is from here, and you two split up."

"Right. We ran into a landslide, and I went ahead on a quad to find a way around the slide." He hadn't mentioned that he had gotten hit in the head and had everything stolen, including the quad. "Tomás is Arturo's brother."

"Our Arturo?"

Chase nodded.

"And Nicole is with your dad on the way to Puebla."

"Or on their way back here if they got word that you and your mother are in Lago." He hadn't mentioned Cindy and Mark. That was way too complicated, and he wasn't sure he understood why they were here himself.

"I'm still confused," Leah said. "Actually I'm shocked. It's not like my dad or my grandmother to let Nicole miss school and her swimming. Weekends are out too. She's a lifeguard at the local pool."

Chase hadn't known Nicole was a lifeguard, but he wasn't surprised. He wished he'd never started this conversation. His mother would have called it a *trie* — not quite the truth, but not exactly a lie. *Nice trie*, she used to tell him.

"I know most of Nicole's friends," Leah continued. "I don't think I've ever met you."

Here we go, Chase thought. "I just moved to Palm Breeze."

"Why would your dad drop everything and come down here to help us?"

"Actually he came down here to help Tomás and his family. It just turned out you were down here too. I guess it was fate."

"Fate, huh?"

Chase shrugged.

"What does your dad do for a living?"

"He . . ." Chase hesitated. "He rescues people."

"That's a job?"

"He used to be a Navy SEAL." Chase wasn't even sure this was true. "Look, your dad said you'd be shocked when Nicole showed up down here. He said to tell you that Momma Rossi was convinced that Nicole had to come with us or bad things would happen."

Leah smiled for the first time. "You should have started with that," she said. "What else did Momma Rossi have to say?"

"Not much," Chase answered, relieved, and wanting badly to keep the smile on Leah's face. "She was a little distracted because of Pet's calf."

"Pet had her baby! Tell me about it!"

Chase described the birth, leaving out anything having to do with the hurricane. Leah's smile broadened with each detail.

"Dad must have been frantic!"

Chase was certain Marco Rossi had been beyond frantic, considering he'd been trying to get back to the farm for Pet's labor during a Category Five hurricane. "He was pretty excited," he said.

Leah's smile turned into a yawn. "Excuse me," she said. "I don't know why I'm so tired. I've been sleeping for hours."

Chase knew exactly why she was tired and hoped she would fall back asleep before she asked any more questions he couldn't answer without *trie-ing*.

"He's definitely in front of us," Nicole said.

"He?" Mark asked.

"The tigers on the show are all males."

They had followed the tracks for at least a hundred feet.

"The question is how far ahead he is." John squatted down to take a closer look at the tracks. "Pugmarks are a little out of my expertise."

"Pugmarks," Mark said. "It would be nice if you guys spoke English."

"*Pug* comes from the Hindi word for 'foot,' " Nicole said.

"Hindi, as in India, where man-eating tigers are from?" Mark asked.

"He's not a man-eater," Nicole said.

"Not yet," Mark said.

"What are the circus tigers like?" John asked.

Nicole looked at the plume. The lightning was still crackling in the black funnel. Out of his cage, in the dark and the wind of Hurricane Emily, the big lion, Simba, had been a completely different cat than he was on the show. Ferocious, aggressive, terrifying. Nicole shuddered.

"They're fine in their cages," she said. "But out here the tiger will be confused, hungry. He may be injured."

"In other words, we're in deep trouble if we run into him," Mark said.

"It would be best if we didn't," Nicole agreed. "Although at some point the circus is going to have to try to get him back. We can't leave a tiger running around Mexico."

John looked ahead into the darkness. "Where do you think the tiger is going?"

Nicole followed John's gaze. "I doubt even he knows."

08:02PM

"I assume none of these houses are yours," Cindy said quietly in Spanish. They were on the final stretch of buckled road leading to the village square.

Tomás walked between the ruins with uncharacteristic slowness, scanning the rubble with his headlamp. "Our home is not here, but these are the homes of my friends. I have seen Popocatepetl erupt many times in my life. There is always damage. This is the worst I have seen."

"Why would anyone live this close to an active volcano?"

"Because it is where we have always lived. The lake provides the water. The mountain provides the floating stones. It is a good place. There is no place that is completely safe."

Cindy couldn't argue with him, but she still thought living in the shadow of an active volcano was tempting fate.

They reached the square.

The only light came from the flickering fires next to where people were sleeping. It was cold. Thunder pealed from the flashing plume.

"A lot of people," Cindy said.

Tomás looked across the broad cobblestoned square at the crude campsites and shelters. "This is only half the people."

He looked beyond the fires and saw the patch of shrouded bodies lined up in neat rows. Next to some of them, people were kneeling. He crossed himself and walked over to where the dead lay.

Father Al saw them approach and stood up from where he was comforting an old woman grieving for her son. He gave Tomás and Cindy a weary smile. "The boy said you would be here."

"Chase?" Cindy said.

"Yes."

"Is he okay?"

"He is fine. He is watching the Rossis in the orphanage. They are badly injured."

Tomás continued to stare at those who were now beyond injury.

Father Al put his hand on Tomás's shoulder. "None of yours are here," he said quietly. "The orphanage was spared. Guadalupe and the children are alive and well."

Tomás nodded stoically, but it was clear that he was greatly relieved. "The generator?" he said.

"Broken," Father Al said. "But it can wait. You and your friend need to rest. You've had a long journey.

"I will fix it now," Tomás said.

08:17 PM

Chase felt a hand on his shoulder and started awake. He turned around. Cindy was standing behind him with her finger to her lips, motioning for him to be quiet. He looked at the Rossis. They were both sound asleep. He stood up. Tomás was not with Cindy, but she wasn't alone. A girl, a few years older than Chase, was standing in the doorway. They walked over to her.

"This is Blanca," Cindy said. "Tomás's oldest daughter."

Chase recognized her from one of the photos on Tomás's dashboard. He gave her a smile and she returned it with a smile of her own.

"Guadalupe is down in the kitchen cooking. Tomás is with her. Blanca will watch the Rossis."

"I don't mind watching them," Chase said.

"Tomás needs your help with the generator."

Chase couldn't imagine Tomás needing help with anything mechanical, but he was pleased to be asked.

As they walked down to the first floor, Cindy explained what had happened since they had separated. Her voice got a little shaky when she came to the part about dangling over the abyss. He knew how she felt. If the pileup had given way when he was crossing it, he would be dead.

Fate, he thought. "So Nicole and my father are okay," he said.

"And Mark," Cindy said.

"Right." He had completely forgotten about the sixth member of their team.

"As far as I know, they are all good. Like I said, the connection was terrible. From what I gathered, they'd found the circus stranded on the road to Puebla. They can't go forward. They can't go back."

"Kind of like us," Chase said.

Cindy nodded. "He said something about elephants and cats getting killed. Apparently, a couple of circus trucks went off the road. I think the drivers died as well. He said *some* of the cats — or *one* of the cats — had escaped. It wasn't clear."

"What kind of cat?"

"I think he said it was a tiger. Your father was afraid he was going to lose the signal, so he was talking fast. He brushed over it like it was no big deal."

That's because he's never come face-to-face with a big cat in the dark, Chase thought.

"Did he say where he thought the tiger was?"

Cindy shook her head. "But just before the signal went dead, he said something about trying to arrange a rescue. I have no idea what he meant by that either."

"Did you tell him about me getting robbed?"

"Yes, and he was very concerned."

"Then he's on his way up here to find me," Chase said.

Cindy looked at him for a moment, then nodded. "I hadn't thought of that, but you're probably right. It's not going to be easy in the dark with essentially no way to get here."

"The only easy day was yesterday," Chase said.

Cindy smiled.

Mark stumbled and fell. He had been walking behind John and Nicole. They ran back and helped him to his feet. He was more concerned about his camera than he was about broken bones.

"I'm fine," he insisted, checking the camera. "I was focusing on the pugmarks, not paying attention to where I was stepping." He turned the camera on and looked through the viewfinder. Satisfied that there was no damage, he turned it off and asked John, "Why are you following the tiger? Aren't we in enough trouble? Things getting a little too dull for you?"

"I'm not following the tiger," John said. "I'm taking the easiest path across the mountain. Apparently, the tiger is doing the same thing."

"He's right," Nicole said. "Cats are generally lazy. This one's taking the path of least resistance."

"Really," Mark said. "Then why did he walk *up* the mountain instead of down?"

John laughed and looked at Nicole. "Mark has a good point."

"I guess," Nicole conceded.

"Here's the deal," John said. "We may bump into the tiger or we may not. It doesn't really matter. We don't have anything to defend ourselves with. We can't outrun it. Therefore the best thing we can do right now is to forget about the tiger. We need to concentrate on getting to Lago. That's our only option."

Mark looked down at the pugmarks. "Or we could walk in the opposite direction."

"You mean walk back down to the road?" John asked.

"Yeah."

"Suit yourself," John said and continued walking in the direction of the pugmarks.

"Mr. Charm," Mark muttered.

Nicole smiled. "Are you really okay?"

"I'm fine. You're the cat expert. What do you do when you run into one in the dark during a volcanic eruption?"

"Cats generally go after the weakest or the slowest."

Mark looked at his camera. "This thing is going to be the death of —"

A lightning bolt struck the ground not twenty feet in front of them. Nicole and Mark were blown off their feet. They landed on their backs with the air knocked out of them.

Nicole raised her head and gulped for breath. The air was filled with the sharp acrid smell of ozone. She wasn't exactly sure what had happened. She sat up.

"Mark?"

"Yeah."

She could barely hear him. It was as if she had cotton stuffed in her ears. And there was something the matter with her vision. Flashes of bright light pulsated across her eyes, making it impossible to see more than a few feet away.

"Did we just get struck by lightning?" Her own voice sounded a mile away from her.

"No," Mark said. "But it was close. Too close. Can you stand up?"

Nicole turned her head, surprised to see that he was right next to her.

"You sound a million miles away."

"Eardrums," he said. "We'll be okay in a little bit. Can you stand?"

"I think so."

She felt him take her hands and pull her to her feet.

"I'm having a hard time seeing," she said.

"That will come back too," Mark said, his voice sounding a little less muffled. "The flash was pretty bright. Blinded me too for a minute, but things are beginning to come into focus again."

"What about —" Nicole began.

"That's my next stop," Mark said. "I'll run up ahead and see how he's doing. He probably didn't even notice that we nearly got hit."

Nicole doubted that.

"Wait here," Mark said.

She wasn't about to wait there. She followed him.

Fifty feet away, they found John Masters lying on the ground. His eyes were closed. He was pale. His right foot was turned at an unnatural angle. Nicole kneeled down next to him.

"He's not breathing," she said.

As Chase and Cindy reached the first floor, the air went still. They stopped and looked at each other.

"The rumbling is gone," Chase said.

Cindy nodded. "I hadn't really noticed the noise until now."

"I wonder what it means," Chase said.

They walked into the kitchen and saw Tomás standing at the window. He was holding two young children in his arms and looking out at Popocatepetl. Guadalupe stood behind him, stirring a delicious-smelling stew on top of a woodstove.

"The moon," Tomás said in English, giving Chase and Cindy a rare smile.

They joined him at the window. The full moon shined brightly next to the plume, casting an eerie light down the mountainside.

"Is it over?" Cindy asked.

Tomás nodded. "For now."

"How do you know?" Chase asked, hoping he was right.

"Experience," Guadalupe answered in surprisingly better English than Tomás spoke. "The worst is behind us. We will mourn our dead, then we will rebuild."

Tomás put the two children down and looked at the bump on Chase's head.

"I'm fine," Chase said.

"Good." He handed Chase his go bag. "We need to fix the generator."

Chase pulled his headlamp out and slipped it on.

The tiger stood listening in the stillness. He looked up at the moon until the ash cloud hid the light. He drank more water. The people were close. He could hear them talking. He was hungry.

08:22PM

"Breathe!" Nicole shouted. She was on her knees next to John Masters, doing rapid and deep chest compressions with the heels of her hands.

"What can I do?" Mark asked, a look of panic and fear on his face.

"Nothing." She stopped the compressions, moved to John's head, tilted it back, filled his lungs with two quick breaths, then started the compressions once again.

Mark paced back and forth. John Masters's luck seemed to have run out. "What are the chances of getting struck by lightning twice?" he shouted in angry frustration. He looked up at the plume, expecting to see more lightning, but the flashes had been replaced by moonlight. The plume seemed to be breaking up, the wind blowing the ash cloud to the east.

And it's quiet, Mark thought. Popocatepetl's roar had stopped. The only thing he could hear was Nicole's rhythmic compressions as she tried to bring Lightning John back to life.

"Breathe!" she shouted again. "Please!"

*　　*　　*

Chase and Cindy followed Tomás out the back door of the orphanage. He led them over to a locked shed. He pulled a key ring out of his pocket and unlocked the double doors. Behind the doors was an impressive collection of tools. Power tools, hand tools, compressors, a portable generator, a welder . . .

Chase smiled. *He has his own private tool stash. Visiting Lago only once a year, it must have taken him years to accumulate all of this stuff.*

Tomás started picking tools off the wall and shelves and putting them into a heavy-duty canvas bag. He looked at Chase and pointed to the portable generator and the dollied acetylene torch used for cutting metal.

Now Chase knew why Tomás had asked for his help. It wasn't to wield tools, it was to haul them.

"I can carry something," Cindy said.

Tomás offered her his go bag.

"Not a chance," she said. She grabbed the dolly with the heavy acetylene and oxygen tanks.

"Breathe!"

John Masters did. His mouth opened. He sucked in a loud gulp of air.

"You saved his life!" Mark shouted.

John stared up at them, disoriented and confused. "What happened?"

"Lightning," Nicole said.

"Again?" John said weakly. He tried to sit up but didn't get very far. He collapsed back onto the ground with a groan.

"I'm afraid I broke, or bruised, some of your ribs giving you CPR."

"Where'd you learn CPR?" John asked weakly.

"Lifeguard class, but I've never had to do it on a real person."

"Thanks," he said hoarsely. "Not for the ribs, but for sav —" He stopped in mid-sentence.

"What's the matter?" Nicole asked, concerned.

"Where's the sound?"

Mark smiled. "While you were taking your catnap, the volcano shut down."

"Catnap, huh?" John laughed, then winced in pain. "How long was I out?"

"You mean dead," Mark said.

"How long?"

Nicole looked at her watch in surprise. "Only four minutes or so," she said. Her arms ached from pushing on his chest.

John tried to sit up again, but it was no good. The pain was too bad.

"Just stay down, for crying out loud," Mark said. "Four minutes is enough to cause brain damage, but apparently it didn't in your case. You're *still* crazy. And Nicole didn't give you the complete diagnosis. Your right leg is broken, or at least twisted up pretty badly. Since you weren't breathing, we didn't think it was important."

"Well, I'm breathing now." John tried to raise his head to see his leg but failed. "Take a look at it."

Nicole and Mark looked without touching it. His right foot was at a right angle to his leg and swelling out of his boot.

"It's your ankle," Mark said. "It looks broken."

"I might be able to set it," Nicole said. "But I'd have to go back down to the tree line to get wood."

"Even if you set it, I wouldn't be able to walk." John laid his head back down and looked up at the sky. He laughed.

"I don't see anything funny about this," Nicole said.

"I'm laughing at your grandmother."

Nicole wondered if John Masters *did* have brain damage after all.

"She told me the lightning was going to find me again," John explained. "I guess she was right." He looked at Nicole. "She also told your father that if you didn't come, something bad was going to happen. I guess she was right about that too. I'd be dead if it weren't for you two."

"I didn't do anything," Mark said.

"I wouldn't say that," John said. "You kept us smiling. That's worth more than you know."

There was something different about John Masters. He wasn't the John Masters from half an hour ago, or even from the day before.

"Are you sure you're okay?" Mark asked.

Nicole was about to ask the same thing. He seemed to have lost his intensity. He looked like Chase's dad and sounded like Chase's dad, but he didn't act like him.

"Aside from my ribs and ankle?" John asked.

"Yeah," Mark said. "You seem . . . I don't know . . . cheerful, I guess."

John thought about it for a moment, then smiled. "I guess you're right. I do feel cheerful. It's been a long time."

"And you do realize that we are stuck on a mountain?"

John nodded. "If this ash went away, we could make a call and get some help. Tomás, Chase, or Cindy might be at Lago by now. I hope they're there."

"The moon was out for a minute," Nicole said. "But the blowing ash has covered it again."

"Where's my go bag?"

It took a while for Mark to find it. The go bag had ended up twenty feet away from where John lay.

"It's totally hammered," Mark said. "Struck by lightning. Everything inside is burned or melted."

"Check your sat phones and see if there's a signal."

They checked and shook their heads.

"That's it, then," John said. "You two go ahead without me. Leave me one of your phones and a bottle of water. If you think about it when you get to Lago, send somebody up here to get me."

"Funny," Nicole said.

"That lightning bolt must have wiped out your short-term memory," Mark said. "There's a tiger wandering around. We can't leave you out here like some kind of roadkill."

"We can't stay here," John said. "Nobody knows where we are. Lago isn't very far."

"I don't feel right about leaving you here," Nicole said. "You're injured."

"I'll go," Mark said. "You stay with John."

"I'll go," Nicole said. "You stay."

"Stop!" John said, some of his former intensity returning. "You're not going by yourself, Nicole. And, Mark, you don't speak Spanish."

"I'm sure someone in Lago speaks enough English for me to make them understand that we need help."

"You're wasting time. No more debate. Give me your phone, Mark."

Mark fished his phone out of his go bag and handed it over. Nicole gave him a bottle of water.

"I still don't feel right about this," Nicole said.

"Just go," John said.

Mark set something down next to him. "What's that?" John asked.

"It's the camera. Keep an eye on it for me."

"Will do," John said.

He listened to them walk away.

Cheerful, he thought. *It's more than that. Content is more like it. That first bolt of lightning took something away from me. Maybe the second one brought something back. I'm so dense, it took not one but two bolts of lightning to square me away.*

He hoped Chase was okay. He was eager to see his son.

*   *   *

The tiger saw the lights and walked toward them. The smell of food was in the dusty air. It was time to eat. Time to drink. Time to find a safe place to rest with a full belly. He heard the human voices. Unfamiliar voices. He was nervous, but he didn't care. Hunger drove his fear away, and his paws toward the dancing lights.

09:02 PM

"There!" Mark said, pointing.

"I see them," Nicole said. Down the mountain, maybe a quarter mile away, several small fires flickered in the dark.

They started down.

"I haven't seen any of those pugmarks in a long time," Mark said.

"I haven't either. He must have gone off in a different direction." Nicole no longer cared about the tiger. Her mother and sister and Chase were close.

The generator was inside the bottling plant, which had been badly damaged by the earthquakes. During the day, when the plant was running, the generator was used to run the pumps and filters and conveyor belts that produced their famous Montaña water. At night and on weekends, when the plant was idle, the generator was used to power the village.

The bottling plant was a lot more sophisticated than Chase had expected it would be. When Father Al had told him about their famous water, he'd had an image of villagers kneeling next to the lake, filling the plastic bottles one at a time, screwing on caps, and tossing them into the back of an old pickup truck. He couldn't have been more wrong. Aside from the church, the bottling plant was easily the largest building in the village. They had entered through a loading-dock door, which had been open when they arrived. Backed up to the dock were three relatively new trucks with the colorful Montaña logo painted on the panels.

A few of the ceiling tiles had fallen and there were thousands of plastic bottles, empty and full, strewn across the floor, making for treacherous walking with the portable generator he was carrying and the acetylene tanks Cindy was pulling. Tomás had tried to take the tanks from her, but she had slapped his hand and told him to quit being ridiculous.

The power plant was in a separate room at the far end of the building. When they got there, Tomás had Chase fire up the portable generator and set up some lights so he could see what he was doing. Tomás started by checking the electrical connections with his ohmmeter.

In the corner was an old sofa. Cindy plopped down on it, and within seconds she was sound asleep.

Chase watched Tomás's clever hands and mind at work, systematically examining the generator from one end to the other. He wondered if Montaña water had existed when Tomás was growing up in the orphanage. He doubted it. The bottled-water craze hadn't been around long. Forty years ago, when Tomás had lived in Lago, they probably really did just scoop water out of the lake.

*   *   *

A villager saw the two lights coming down the mountain and alerted Father Al. He and a small group of men met Nicole and Mark just before they reached the square. Nicole quickly explained who they were and what had happened to John Masters.

"How far up the mountain is he?" Father Al asked.

"Two miles," Mark said. "Three at the most."

Father Al asked two of the men to go into the church and get a stretcher. "You say he was struck by lightning."

"Yes," Nicole said.

"And he lived."

"That's right," Mark said. "And that's not the first time he's been struck."

"A miracle," Father Al muttered, and crossed himself.

"Are my mother and sister here?" Nicole asked, almost afraid to hear his answer.

"Oh, yes," Father Al said. "They are in the orphanage, asleep. They have been injured."

"How badly?"

"Your mother is worse off than your sister, but if we can get her to a hospital soon, I think she will recover."

Nicole looked at Mark. He smiled. "Don't worry about it. I'll take them up to retrieve Lightning John."

"Thank you, Mark." She gave him a hug, then turned to the priest. "Where's the orphanage, Father?"

"Behind the church, but please try not to wake them. At this point, sleep is the best medicine. In fact, it is our only medicine until we get them to a proper facility."

Nicole smiled and started toward the square, but she didn't get far. She froze in mid-step.

"Oh, no!"

"What?" Mark hurried over and looked down. He swore.

Father Al joined them but didn't understand what they were staring at on the ground.

"There's a tiger in the village," Nicole said as calmly as she could. "We need to get everyone into the church until we find out where it is."

Tomás waved Chase over and showed him a handful of fuses. "In the shed," he said. "In a red box. Bring the box."

Chase smiled. He had always liked Tomás's way of communicating.

Clear and concise.

"I'll bring them right back."

He headed out of the generator room toward the loading dock, happy to have something to do, and hoping that the fix was as simple as a new fuse.

An odd sensation overcame him as he walked past the conveyor belt. He stopped. The hair on the back of his neck prickled. He felt the same unpleasant sensation he had felt not two days before. Something was watching him. He could feel its eyes on him.

It can't be.

He slowly moved his headlamp around the huge room. Bottles, boxes, equipment, and enough shadows to hide an elephant.

It's my imagination. I'm just tired. I'm having a flashback.

But he knew none of this was true. There was a tiger in the building.

Nicole had told him that the most important thing was containment, but he didn't think she meant to contain the animal in the same container you're standing in. At the farm, they'd had a shotgun and a tranquilizer. Now he had nothing.

Cindy and Tomás have less than nothing. They don't know the tiger is here.

He looked behind him. The light shined through the generator door. He looked in front of him at the loading-dock door.

Midway.

If he made a run for the generator room and slammed the door, the tiger could leave the building. There were people in the square. The church door was open. The orphanage door was open. The tiger could go wherever it wanted.

The loading-dock door was a roll-up with a pull chain on the side. If he managed to get there without getting mauled, the tiger would be between him and the open generator door. Cindy was sound asleep. And Tomás might not understand if Chase shouted for him to close the door. Besides, Chase knew him well. Tomás wouldn't close the door without an explanation. If he thought Chase was in trouble, he would step out into the open and take on whatever it was.

Not even Tomás's clever hands can stop a tiger.

"What are the chances of this happening twice?" he asked himself. "About as likely as being struck by lightning twice. Paranoia. I'm being ridiculous."

Just then he heard the crunch of something heavy stepping on empty plastic bottles. He turned his headlamp in time to see the flash of a striped tail disappearing into the shadows.

They managed to get everyone into the church without too much panic. Most of the villagers believed they were being herded inside because of the volcano.

It was crowded, with the injured taking up most of the pews. Father Al closed the double doors and started up the center aisle to the pulpit. Nicole and Mark stood at the back.

"What about John?" Mark asked.

"I guess he's going to have to wait until we get this figured out. I doubt anyone is going to want to go outside with a tiger loose." She tried to spot Chase or Tomás in the dark church, but it was nearly impossible to see anyone in the candlelit room. "As soon as Father Al's finished, we'll look for Chase, Tomás, and Cindy. Between the five of us, we'll be able to get John down here."

Father Al spoke in Spanish. Nicole translated for Mark.

"Thank you for being calm," he said, his deep voice filling the large church. "I believe that Popocatepetl has gone back to sleep. It was a terrible day. I am sorry for your losses. But right now we have another problem. I have asked you to come in here because we believe there is a circus tiger loose in the village."

Alarm and disbelief spread throughout the church. Father Al let them express their dismay for nearly a minute before holding up his hands to silence them.

"We believe everyone is in here, or inside the orphanage. We are safe as long as we stay inside and stay calm."

"How will we get the tiger?" a man shouted.

"We are working on that," Father Al said. "I'm going to go over to the orphanage to talk to the circus people and find out what we can do about our visitor."

"The only circus people who are healthy are clowns!" another man shouted.

"There is an animal trainer among them," Father Al said.

"A poodle trainer," someone else shouted.

Some people wailed. Others laughed.

"This is not going well," Nicole said. She started toward the aisle.

Mark caught up with her. "What are you going to do?"

"I'm going to talk to the congregation," Nicole answered. She reached the pulpit and whispered something in Father Al's ear. He nodded and stepped aside.

Nicole waited for everyone to quiet down, which didn't take long. They stared up at her with curiosity and confusion. Public speaking had never been Nicole's favorite subject in school. Now she had to speak to over a hundred people in Spanish.

"My name is Nicole Rossi. My parents own the Rossi Brothers' Circus. There was a terrible accident on the road to Puebla. Two trucks went off the road. Five of my friends were killed, along with all of our elephants and our lions and tigers . . . except one. He managed to escape. I am sorry for this. I am also sorry for the loss of my friends and the animals."

A tear rolled down her cheek. She paused and gathered herself before continuing.

"The clowns and the dog trainer have been with the circus for many years. During those years, they have seen many things and worked with many different animals. If the tiger is in Lago, we will find him and contain him before he harms anyone. You have my word."

She looked out into the dark church. No one said a word. She turned to Father Al and said quietly, "I need to talk to my friends."

"They are in the orphanage with your mother and sister," Father Al said. "I haven't had time to tell them about the tiger."

"I'll tell them," Nicole said. "I assume that Chase, Tomás, and Cindy are over there too?"

Father Al went a little pale. He shook his head. "They are in the bottling plant, trying to fix the generator."

Chase needed to make up his mind. The rattling of the bottles was getting louder. Tomás was going to hear the noise and come out to investigate. Chase turned around very slowly and faced the generator door.

"Tomás!" he yelled.

The rattling stopped. He wished it hadn't.

Tomás appeared in the doorway, looking concerned.

"You need to close the door! The tiger is in here. I am going to make a run for the loading dock."

Tomás took a step out.

"No!" Chase shouted. "Stay where you are!"

Tomás hesitated.

A sleepy-looking Cindy appeared behind him. "What's going on?"

"The tiger is in the building. You need to close the generator door. I'm going to try to get to the loading dock and close that door so it doesn't escape into the village. You cannot come out until I tell you it's safe."

"But —"

"I'll be fine, and so will you if you stay where you are. Close the door. Now!"

Cindy quickly explained the situation to Tomás. After a long moment's hesitation, he closed the door slowly. Now the only light in the plant came from Chase's headlamp. What he had not told Cindy was that the dock door could be closed only by the chain from inside. He would have to pull the heavy door down, then find the small door to the side to get out.

The ground floor of the orphanage was chaotic. Poodles barking, children crying, people talking over one another.

"What are you doing here, Nicole?"

"Which tiger is it?"

"The elephants are dead?"

"Who was driving the trucks?"

"Enough!" Nicole said. "We need to find our friends and tell them about the tiger. Then we need to search the village to find out if it is still here."

"Yes, we will all go," Pierre Deveroux, the dog trainer, said. "We will walk in a large group with sticks or whatever we can find. It is unlikely the tiger will attack a group."

"Unlikely," Dennis the clown said.

Pierre shrugged. "Nothing is for certain of course."

"Of course," Mark said.

Dennis smiled.

"If we can, we will contain him," Pierre said. "If we cannot, we will try to drive him from the village."

Chase ran toward the door, but he didn't get very far. He slipped on the bottles and fell.

This is it! American boy mauled to death by tiger in bottled-water plant in Mexico.

But that wasn't it. The big cat sounded like it was having the same difficulty negotiating the bottles strewn across the floor as Chase had.

The tiger roared in frustration.

Chase stood back up. He started moving forward again, but this time he went more slowly, trying to be careful about where he put his feet. He risked a glance behind him and wished he hadn't. The tiger was out in the open now and gaining on him.

Concentrate on the chain!

Chase wanted to head straight through the door and run off into the dark night, but it was too late for that. If the tiger followed him, he would never be able to outrun it. His only hope was the door, and the ruse Momma Rossi had used to confuse Hector the leopard back in Florida.

Chase lunged for the chain and grabbed it with his right hand, hoping the door hadn't been left open because it was broken. With his left hand he tore the headlamp off his forehead and tossed it back toward where he thought the tiger was. He was working in complete darkness now. The door began to close as Chase double-handed the chain down as fast as he could. The tiger growled. The light from Chase's headlamp flashed around the building, which meant the tiger had fallen for Momma Rossi's trick. The door clicked shut as it smashed into the threshold. The headlamp went out. The tiger had snapped the bulb.

All I have to do now is crawl a dozen feet to my left, find the small door in the pitch dark, and let myself out before the tiger pounces on me.

He started to crawl.

The tiger ran into the big metal door and let out another horrendous growl.

Chase tried to ignore the terrible sound as he felt his way along the wall. The building was made of cinder blocks. He felt the metal doorframe.

Doorknob. Four feet up from the ground.

He reached for where he thought the doorknob should be, but just then the door swung open. A hand reached through and pulled him to the dock. A second later, the tiger hit the door. The door held.

Gasping for breath, Chase looked up at his savior. It was Tomás. He helped Chase to his feet, then took a close look at him as if he were checking to see if Chase still had all of his limbs.

"You okay?"

"No," Chase said. "How did you get here?"

"Window," Tomás answered.

Chase started laughing. Tomás joined him.

And that's how Nicole, Mark, Cindy, and the others found them.

"You two have a really twisted sense of humor," Mark said.

Nicole looked at the doors. She could hear the tiger on the other side. "Did you catch yourself another cat?"

"Sure did," Chase said. He looked at Tomás. "With a little help from my friend. Where's my dad?"

"Up on the mountain," Nicole said.

"Taking a catnap," Mark said. "Guess we should go up there and wake him."

10:47 PM

Chase was the first to reach his father.

"Hey, sport," his father said.

"What time is it?" Chase asked.

His father laughed. "You know what? I have no idea. Apparently, that last bolt knocked the ability right out of me. I guess I'll have to buy a watch now."

"You okay?"

"A couple cracked ribs and a badly sprained ankle."

"Mark said he thought it was broken."

"I bet you he's wrong."

Nicole and Cindy came up next, followed by Tomás, Mark, and several men from the village with a stretcher.

His father's sat phone rang, startling everyone.

"Excuse me," he said, and answered it. "That's a negative. The cavalry just arrived. They're taking me down the mountain as we speak. Go ahead and evac the circus people. I'll get an LZ cleared up here and see you at the village at first light. Roger that. Out."

"Who was that?" Chase asked.

"That was SEAL Team One commander Raul Delgado."

"The only easy day was yesterday," Chase said.

His father smiled. "As it turns out, you might be right. I guess I have some explaining to do."

"Yeah, you do," Chase said.

"And I promise I will," his father said. He turned to Nicole. "Most of your people are on army trucks headed back to Mexico City. Delgado is going to move the animals next. Road crews should have the slide cleared and the bridge back up in a few days, and they'll be able retrieve their vehicles then. Delgado is leaving a couple men behind to keep an eye on things until they can return."

He handed Mark the video camera.

Mark turned it on and started filming.

Dawn filtered through the window as Tomás tightened the last bolt. He passed the ratchet to Chase, then wiped his clever hands with a rag.

"Fixed?" Chase asked.

"Maybe."

They had been in the generator room since they'd dropped Chase's father at the church to have his ribs and ankle looked at. When Chase wasn't handing Tomás tools, he was at the metal door peering through the safety glass. It was too dark to see the bottling plant, but he could hear the tiger prowling, slapping plastic bottles across the cement floor.

Tomás hit some switches and the generator came to life. The tiger roared.

Chase hurried over to the door. The tiger had his front paws on the conveyor belt and was looking up at the fluorescent lights.

Contained, Chase thought. *And bigger than he looked last night.*

He walked back over to Tomás.

"Everything good?"

"I think."

"I'm going over to the church to check on my dad."

Tomás nodded. "I will watch the generator."

"Don't open the door," Chase said, smiling.

Tomás laughed.

Chase climbed through the window. The sun was rising over the top of Popocatepetl. The slopes were covered with ash. A wisp of white steam curled up from the crater. The mountain was peaceful once again, but the memory of its violence was everywhere as Chase made his way to the village square.

He arrived just as the first chopper touched down on the cobblestones in a swirl of ash. His father was on crutches, waiting for it. Mark had his camera rolling. Cindy stood by him, jotting something down in a notebook. Chase stood at the edge of the square, out of the worst of the ash, and watched.

A big man in a black uniform jumped out, walked up to Chase's father, and saluted. John returned the salute.

Commander Delgado.

Chase shook his head. *I guess I had to see it to believe it*, he thought. *Dad really was a Navy SEAL.*

Several other men jumped out of the chopper, carrying stretchers and supplies. The last two men to climb out were not dressed in uniforms. One was tall and thin. The other was squat and heavy. They carried a large crate between them.

Circus roustabouts.

Nicole came out of the church alongside the stretcher carrying her mother. Leah's stretcher was right behind them.

Chase waved, but Nicole didn't notice. She was talking to her mother. The men loaded the stretchers onto the chopper, and Nicole climbed in after them.

I should go up and say something. I can't just let her fly off. Chase started forward, but stopped. More stretchers were arriving. He didn't want to get in their way. He looked at his father, who was laughing about something with Delgado and Cindy. Mark was still filming. *Nicole wouldn't leave without saying good-bye.* Another chopper appeared over the lake and hovered, awaiting its turn. Two more stretchers were brought out to the first chopper. *Now or never.* He started across the square. Nicole jumped off the chopper before he had taken ten steps. He stopped again. She waved to someone inside and hurried out from beneath the rotors.

"Nicole!"

She ran over and gave him a hug.

"You're not going with your mom and sister?"

She shook her head. "I didn't want to take the space from someone who's injured. I'm taking the last chopper out with the poodles and the tiger." She raised an eyebrow. "You didn't think I'd leave without saying good-bye, did you?"

"Well . . ."

Nicole took his hand. "Let's go down to Lago de la Montaña. I haven't seen it yet."

07:56 AM

Nicole and Chase walked along the shore, holding hands.

"So your mom's okay," Chase said.

Nicole nodded. "She woke up last night, wanting to get out of bed to check on the animals. It took three of us to hold her down. Leah wasn't much better. Rossis aren't very good at lying around. The doctor had been worried about spine or neck injuries, but he revised his prognosis after seeing her trying to get up. He suggested she stay in the hospital for several days. I predict it will be one day at the most. I talked to my dad. He's on the same flight we took to Mexico City. With any luck, he'll beat them to the hospital and try to keep them in their beds for a couple of days."

"Who's taking care of the farm?"

"The Stones. I talked to Rashawn. Pet and the calf are fine. The only problem they're having is with her little brother. He's so excited to be around the animals that Momma Rossi's threatening to lock him up in one of the cages so he doesn't hurt himself."

The second chopper took off and a third landed.

"Have they picked up the people on the road?" Chase asked.

"They're all at the fairgrounds with Arturo. As soon as I show up with the tiger, we'll head back to the States."

"Then what?"

Nicole shook her head. "I don't know. It could be the end of the Rossi Brothers' Circus. But you never know. We've been through bad times and the show still went on. We have all winter to see where we're at." She stopped and picked up a piece of pumice. "What about you?" she asked. "What are your plans?"

"I don't know. I haven't had a chance to talk to my father. It's up to him."

"You're welcome to come back with me to the farm. We could use your help and I . . ." She flushed and looked away. "So tell me about that tiger."

Chase smiled, but it wasn't about the tiger. He was pretty certain that Nicole felt the same way about him as he did about her.

"What's so funny?"

"Not a thing."

Chase leaned forward and kissed her.

09:30 AM

The last chopper had landed. They were standing outside the bottling plant.

"I guess it's tiger time," Nicole said. She looked at Chase. "So you think I can tranquilize it from the generator room?"

Chase nodded. "There's a small safety window in the door. It will have to be broken out to get the rifle through, but Tomás is there. He can break it out for you."

"All right," Nicole said. "Let's get this over with."

Commander Delgado looked at Nicole and scratched his stubbled chin. "I'll just come out with it," he said. "You can say yes or no. It's totally up to you. You're the expert. You're the boss. But I have always wanted to dart a big cat. Can I dart the big fella?"

Nicole looked at him and squinted her eyes. "What kind of shot are you?"

Delgado gave her a big smile. Chase's father smiled too. "Well, I'm a pretty fair shot, truth be told. But I'll be honest — I've never shot a tranquilizer rifle like this one."

Nicole looked at John. "What do you think?"

"He did fly out here and rescue your mom and sister and ferry all the circus people to the other side of the bridge."

"Don't forget the animals," Delgado said. "We took them too. Getting those camels on the chopper was no picnic, I can tell you. Although it was kind of fun."

Nicole handed him the rifle. "Okay. You need to hit the large muscle mass in the hind leg. Seventy-five to a hundred feet max."

"I'm not going in there without you," Delgado said. "You need to guide me through it."

They disappeared around the corner, with Mark and Cindy close behind. That left Chase and his father alone.

"You're sure your ankle isn't broken?" Chase asked.

"Just a bad sprain. The crutches make it look worse than it is."

"And the ribs?"

"Those do hurt, but they'll heal."

"You won't be much good around here stove-in like you are."

"I'll supervise Tomás."

Chase laughed. "Like he needs you telling him what to do."

"Good point, but I'm still going to stick around. For a while anyway."

"Did they get that guy on the road with the broken leg?"

"The guy who hit you in the head and hijacked the quad?"

"Yeah, that guy."

"They got him, but it wasn't easy. No place to land. They had to rope him up."

"Good." Chase was in a forgiving mood.

"Are you heading out with Nicole and the tiger? I talked to Marco. He said he would be happy to have you stay on the farm a while. I'm sure Nicole would too."

Chase grinned. "I think I'd better stay here with you."

"What about school?"

"It'll be a couple of weeks before they get the schools going in Palm Breeze again."

"Then what?"

"You tell me," Chase said.

His father shook his head. "No, Chase, you tell *me*. When we're done here, we can go back to Palm Breeze. We can even go back home if you want."

"Oregon?" Chase was shocked.

His father held his gaze for a moment. "I'm ready, Chase."

Chase wasn't sure that *he* was ready. He'd put that possibility out of his mind a long time ago. And now there was Nicole to think about. "Are you sure you're okay? Did the lightning strike —"

"Knock some sense into me?"

"I guess. I mean you're acting like you did before —" He didn't finish the sentence. It was a subject they never talked about.

His father finished the sentence for him. "Before your mom and Little Monkey died?"

Chase hadn't heard his father use his sister Monica's nickname since the accident.

"I'm better, Chase. No more storm running. No more running from myself. It's my turn to follow you."

"The only *hard* day was yesterday?" Chase said.

"Let's hope so." His father smiled and put his hand out. "Do we have a deal?"

Chase shook his father's hand, happy to have him back, but wondering how long it would last.

"Deal," he said.